THE KILLING PAGES

A DCI LUKE WILEY BOOK

JAYE BAILEY

Also by Jaye Bailey

The DCI Luke Wiley Thrillers

A Grave Return

The Quiet and the Dead

The Killing Pages

A Spirit in the Dark

PROLOGUE

She was a full twenty minutes late. And she was late on purpose.

Lisa was never late and she found this tardiness almost painful. Her mother's voice still rang in her head, even at the age of thirty six. *Do you think your time is more valuable than anyone else's?*

Lisa wasn't actually late. She was standing around the corner from the restaurant she was supposed to have arrived at twenty minutes earlier, and she had been standing there killing time for what felt like much longer than that. She pulled her phone out of her pocket and looked at the time yet again.

If her mother could see her now, hovering on a random side street in this busy pocket of London, making a man wait for her, she would probably be pleased. The lessons passed on from her mother weren't exactly about Lisa's self-worth, or about her general happiness or well-being. Her mother used to tell her that the only way to get what she wanted from a man was to play him. Men needed to be aroused and toyed with and manipulated just slightly so that you were able to always have the upper hand.

Lisa loathed this advice from her mother. When she was younger, she couldn't bear the thought of a game plan when it came to relationships. She thought that honesty and the matching of similar interests and a healthy dose of physical attraction would be the basis of her life going forward.

And then she found herself getting divorced at thirty five.

Her mother wasn't able to say *I told you so*, but only because she had died a few years earlier.

The divorce hadn't come as a massive shock to Lisa. The relationship had become stale. She suspected that her husband's eyes and desires were elsewhere and the fact that he had at least had the decency to ask for a separation before jumping into bed with someone else was admirable.

But Lisa had been left feeling hurt and exhausted and a little bit lonely by the entire thing. After a year, her remaining single friends encouraged her to join them in the terrifying world of online dating and she had thought *why the hell not*.

What did she have to lose?

She hadn't been single for over a decade and assembling an online dating profile was, she had to admit, a lot of fun. She was ready for a bit of reinvention and how better to do that than to curate exactly the kind of person she wanted to be by answering a series of questions on a screen. Part of her felt like she was being interviewed for a profile piece in the Times, and she spent hours concocting the perfect responses. And uploaded the perfect photos to match.

It was thrilling to see so many eligible bachelors liking her profile and her self-esteem ramped up a few notches. No longer did she feel like Lisa, the woman in her mid-thirties that her ex-husband had described as "lovely but uninspiring" when they had separated. She felt like she had everything to offer and vowed to be extra discerning with her choice of date as a result.

The evening her phone chimed with an alert from the dating app and the smiling face of Trevor (forty, likes Scandinavian crime box sets, lawyer so unfortunately spends too much time in the office but makes up for it by weekends away in Europe, favourite place to visit is Italy which he should say is because of the art and the history but really the food just tastes better in Italia!) beamed up at her, she took just a second to swipe right. He messaged back immediately and so began the most exciting few weeks of her life for the past several years.

Lisa felt awful making him wait in the restaurant for her. And she was freezing by this point. The early December weather in London wasn't as cold as it could be, but she also wasn't dressed for it. Or at least not dressed to be standing outside for twenty minutes in this weather pretending to be late. She could have thrown on her warmer winter coat, but the thin grey felt cape looked fantastic with her dress and long black boots. She knew that she looked fabulous, in a way that she hoped looked effortless, and after one more glance at her phone, she started walking towards the restaurant.

Lisa had waited a few dates before sleeping with Trevor. She wasn't exactly sure of the protocol of sex in a new relationship, and if that was now different a good decade after she had last been dating, or if being in her mid-thirties had also changed the rules.

There are no rules, her friend had said. Just go with what you're feeling. And for god's sake, just have fun. Don't overthink it.

So she didn't overthink it and the entire evening had seemed perfect. It was a Saturday evening and Trevor had invited her over for dinner at his flat. Her mobile had rung around four o'clock that afternoon and she could see that it was Trevor calling. Her heart sank as she worried that he was calling to cancel, and she had been looking forward to that night being the night — a progression in their relationship from casual dating to perhaps something a little more concrete.

But Trevor wasn't calling to cancel. He had been watching the football with a friend and realized that he hadn't thought about what to cook for dinner. He was going to pop into Borough Market and pick up some groceries. Would Lisa like to meet him there around five thirty and they could choose what to cook together? Maybe stop for a glass of wine on the way back to his flat?

Lisa was slightly stunned at this phone call. It was so thoughtful and casual and the fact that he wanted to spend more time with her than just a quick, convenient dinner at his flat made her almost a little bit giddy. She said that she thought it was a great idea and she'd see him there.

Thank god I washed my hair and shaved my legs this morning, Lisa thought, as she checked the time and calculated how long she had to get ready for the evening and then out the door to get to the south end of London.

The afternoon of shopping for food — they went with mussels and fresh crusty sourdough, along with half a dozen different cheeses for afterwards — and the evening that followed were as she had hoped they would be. They were relaxed, warm, full of conversation and laughter and all apprehension Lisa felt about taking her clothes off in front of a man she hadn't known very long fell away.

As she lay in Trevor's arms afterwards, she felt something that she hadn't felt in a long time. She felt happy.

When Lisa woke, the room was still dark and she could feel that she was alone in the bed. Turning over and easing herself out from under the covers, she stepped towards the window and pulled back the heavy curtain to let a bit of light into the bedroom. It had been dark when she arrived at Trevor's flat the

previous evening and she hadn't been able to see the view from
the top floor of the old listed building he lived in. The flat was
a couple of blocks back from the Thames, which you could
just see over the tops of the buildings between the one she was
in and the river. It was a lovely view, even on a dark late
November morning.

Lisa looked around the room for a mirror but there wasn't
one and the bathroom was outside in the hallway. She
wondered how long Trevor had been awake and she stood still
to see if she could hear any movement in the flat. Perhaps he
was making breakfast to bring back to her in bed, although she
couldn't smell anything coming from the kitchen.

She opened the bedroom door and could suddenly hear
the faint noise of the news coming from either the television
or the radio. She slipped into the bathroom and freshened up a
bit, noticing how cute Trevor's t-shirt, handed to her to sleep
in the night before, looked on her. It hung just off one
shoulder and fell to the top of her thighs. Tousling her hair
one more time, she walked into the kitchen to see if she could
help with breakfast.

Except Trevor had already eaten. And he was dressed.

Lisa had this all wrong. He clearly wasn't coming back to
bed to spend the morning with her.

She quickly surveyed the scene in front of her. Trevor was
showered and in jeans and a green collared shirt, fastening his
watch strap and staring at the open laptop on the kitchen
island in front of him. To the side of his laptop was a bowl that
looked like it had contained berries and yogurt. An empty
mug sat next to the espresso machine, which had been used
and then switched off again.

Not only was Trevor not coming back to bed, it looked
like he was about to head out the door and wanted Lisa out of
the flat as well.

She was slightly stunned, embarrassed that she had read the situation so wrong and she couldn't bring herself to even say good morning. She stood limply at the entrance to the kitchen, just staring at him.

'Hey,' he said, smiling at her. 'Look, I'm really sorry but I actually have to go into the office.'

'Oh. Okay.'

'So sorry. Something has come up and it can't wait until tomorrow.'

'Sure,' Lisa said. 'No problem.'

Did she sound too curt when she said this? She meant it to sound casual, but it was almost impossible for her voice to pull this off. She was startled and she was hurt. And she wanted to get the hell out of there.

The rest of that Sunday had felt bad enough, but then Lisa hadn't heard from Trevor for over three weeks. She had commiserated with her friends and tried to snap out of the funk she had fallen into, but it had been hard. Something that she thought had gone so well had clearly not gone well at all.

She could hear her mother's words in her head.

So when a text popped up on her mobile three days ago from Trevor, asking if she was free for dinner, she took a good couple of hours to text back.

What did this mean? Was he trying to make amends for the abrupt ending to their last date? Had he been seeing someone else in the meantime and wanted to tell her? Was he after just another hook up? Did he want to simply try one more time because she had been bad in bed that night?

Now she was overthinking and she decided, for once, to take her dead mother's advice which was the first time she had ever done so. What did she have to lose at this point? It wasn't as if her mother was going to say I told you so if this approach worked.

So Lisa made Trevor wait and as she approached the restaurant, a gorgeous little bistro in Bloomsbury on a small street of restaurants on one side and stores on the other, with a few houses at the very end of the block, she could see him sitting in front of the restaurant in a sort of halo of light. The bistro looked busy and he was on a stool at the counter that ran the length of the window, a half drunk glass of white wine in front of him and what looked like a folded newspaper.

It looked like he was patiently waiting for her. Lisa took this to be a good sign.

Trevor looked up as she walked across the street. He swiveled off his stool and opened the door for her. Lisa couldn't help but smile and as Trevor kissed her gently on the lips, her stomach flipped over. It was such a public display of affection. Another good sign.

Trevor slipped the grey cape off Lisa's shoulders and as she turned from him to release her arms from the fabric, she bit the inside of her cheek to remind herself to calm down and play it cool.

'It's great to see you,' Trevor said.

'I'm so sorry I'm late. I got caught up,' Lisa lied.

Trevor smiled at her.

'It's not a problem. I'm afraid I ordered myself a glass of wine while I was waiting. They do have our table ready, which is at the back there,' Trevor pointed to the corner of the room, 'but if you want to sit up at the counter here, it's actually quite cozy.'

'Sure, why not?' Lisa shrugged, thinking that they were sitting much closer together on these little stools. It was perfect.

Two more glasses of wine were ordered and they chatted amiably for a few minutes. Trevor asked how Lisa's pitch had gone at work, a full two weeks ago now, but Lisa was pleased he had remembered. The conversation was light, but comfortable.

'Look,' Trevor finally said. 'I want to apologize for the last time we saw each other. I imagine that I made you feel unwelcome that morning and it wasn't my intention.'

'Oh don't worry,' Lisa said, her hand fluttering in front of her, as if she was trying to swipe away the memory of the awkward encounter so it never existed at all.

'No, I really want to apologize. Sometimes I'm not great at communication and I'm afraid I woke up that morning to a very tense series of emails from my managing partner and I just needed to get into the office to deal with it. But it had absolutely nothing to do with you and I wouldn't want you to think that I had a bad time that night.'

Trevor leaned forward and squeezed her knee under the counter.

'Because I didn't,' he continued. 'And I'd really like to pick up where we left off, if you're not too irritated by my behaviour. Which you have every right to be.'

Trevor picked up his wine glass and took a sip from it, his eyebrows raised in a cute, pleading kind of way.

Lisa reached across the counter and touched his hand, banishing all thoughts of her mother from her head.

'All is forgiven. Honestly. I've been busy too, and hadn't really been thinking about it.'

One last lie and then they could move on. It seemed to do the trick.

'Great,' said Trevor. 'Shall we order? Believe it or not, the mussels are supposed to be very good here.'

Lisa laughed and was smoothing a piece of her hair down around her ear when a car backfired just outside the restaurant on the street. She jumped and grabbed the counter with one hand, while the other involuntarily flew up to her chest in surprise.

She was about to make a joke when she saw Trevor's face clouded with confusion, staring at the window in front of them. Lisa looked through the window at the street to see what he was staring at, and then realized that it was the window itself he was studying. The glass just in front of her had cracked in a circular pattern, like a spider web.

The car backfired again and this time Lisa was so shocked she stumbled backwards off her stool, grasping onto the counter as she began to fall. The woman sitting next to her further down the counter screamed and Lisa turned towards her.

At that moment, the window suddenly exploded, shards of glass launching into the air around them. The noise was deafening and Lisa's ears were ringing, as if she had just left a loud concert. She shook her head to try to clear them, and she looked towards Trevor.

He wasn't there.

Lisa thought that she had lost her hearing, but then the woman shouted out again and she realized that the room had actually been enveloped in silence.

'You're bleeding,' the woman cried out to Lisa.

'What?'

'Oh my god, oh my god,' the woman was shouting.

'I'm calling an ambulance,' she heard a man say behind her.

Lisa looked first at her hands, which were covered in blood. It was a shocking red, and it wouldn't stop coming. Her hands were still clutching her chest and her shoulder suddenly felt both hot and numb at the same time. *Where had Trevor gone*, Lisa thought.

Everyone in the restaurant was standing and she couldn't see what was happening. A man rushed over to her and pressed his cloth napkin against her chest. The white fabric turned crimson and the man told her to lie down and that help was on the way.

As Lisa was lowered to the floor she saw Trevor. A man was crouched over him performing CPR and then he suddenly stopped. She could see why.

The bullet had gone right through his neck. He would have been dead before he hit the ground.

ONE

L uke Riley was off duty. Exactly three days ago he had stood in his bedroom in his house in London, an empty duffle bag on the bed in front of him, as he decided what he needed to pack. The result was not much at all.

He wasn't off on a long haul flight or a hot beach destination. Instead, Luke was driving out to his cottage in the Cotswolds to spend a full seven days doing his best not to think about work. Not terribly exciting to most, but for Luke's mood at the moment, it was the perfect week.

The last few weeks between finding Caitlin Black and Poppy Travis had felt like a slog. It often happened like this. There was the euphoria that came along with the conclusion of a particularly tough case, and the death of Grace Feist which led to the discovery of Caitlin Black being alive all of these years and then rescuing Poppy Travis when she was kidnapped, was an enormous relief. The atmosphere on the Serious Crime Unit on the seventh floor of New Scotland Yard was almost electric. Rowdy had commented that anyone with sensitive hearing could probably get the specific decibel of the buzz that permeated the entire floor.

And then following every euphoric moment comes the inevitable crash. For Luke this happened quite quickly as Hana returned to work a little too quickly for his liking, and didn't seem herself. How could she?

Hana Sawatsky could take a lot on the job, but she had been attacked and held prisoner. Even if it was for just a few hours, the ordeal had taken its toll.

'How are you feeling?' Luke had kept asking her, until she finally snapped at him.

'How did you feel when people kept asking you this question after Sadie died?' she spat at him in the corridor one morning.

Luke quietly apologized and slinked back to his office. Hana had popped her head in later that day to apologize herself.

'I'm sorry. I shouldn't have said that. Completely different circumstances.'

Luke waved off her apology. He was worried about her and to be honest, a bit desperate for everything to feel like it usually felt between them. What exactly that was like was hard to explain, but he was missing it.

After two weeks of Luke and Hana dragging themselves through the working week, it was actually Chief Superintendent Stephen O'Donnell who suggested they both take a bit of time off. This benevolent gesture had, to put it mildly, been a surprise to them both.

When Luke had questioned O'Donnell about this unexpected suggestion, O'Donnell had explained that they could afford a bit of reduced manpower and as the holiday season was rapidly approaching, the detectives might be needed then. There had been no argument from Luke or Hana and that's how Luke found himself wondering what to put in his duffle bag just a few days later.

His laptop, a spare jumper and pair of jeans, as well as a smarter jacket and collared shirt, just in case he was asked to dinner by a neighbour, were thrown into the bag. And there was one more thing he craved.

On his way downstairs, bag over his shoulder, he popped into the room that was once Sadie's study. The room was never used as an office particularly, as Sadie had sold her company and no longer worked full-time when she renovated this house. Instead, the room was fitted with a low, sleek gas fireplace and one entire wall fitted with floor to ceiling bookshelves. There was no desk, but instead a couple of large chairs you could sink your whole body into, even when crosslegged, and an oversized coffee table between them. Sadie used to come in here to spend hours on her laptop with her various charitable interests — she had served on a number of boards — but primarily, she liked to read crime novels. They took up most of the space on these bookshelves. There were hundreds of them. Every series was arranged in sequential order, but the authors weren't in alphabetical alignment on the shelves. Sadie liked to place them in order of theme — cozy crime, gritty crime, particular detectives she enjoyed, the classic mystery books, the ones set in Scotland or Canada or the Lake District.

Luke didn't truly understand the system, but it didn't matter. He liked to dip in and pick a novel at random, most often by the title that appealed to him. There were a couple of series that he liked more than others, and he had to absolve every error made in the police procedural ones, but reading these books made it feel, even if just for a moment, that Sadie was still in the room next to him.

He hadn't had the time to be able to spend an entire afternoon just reading one of these in many weeks, so Luke was looking forward to losing himself in these pages. He selected two books — each from a different part of the bookshelf — and slipped them into his bag.

When he arrived at Bluffs Cottage not having been there for some time, the house was freezing and the power had clearly gone out at some point, which had tripped a couple of fuses so only some lights were on and the digital clocks on the appliances in the kitchen were flashing at him.

Luke had a momentary wave of regret. Should he have come out to the cottage instead of actually getting away? And somewhere warm?

There were certain moments when he missed his wife more than others and opening up Bluffs Cottage was one of them. Sadie would have sorted everything so quickly and her knack for getting a fire started and roaring in a cold wood stove was not a skill that Luke possessed. He felt a little on the melancholy side for the rest of the evening.

But in daylight and with the week stretched out ahead of him, Luke settled into a comfortable rhythm in the cottage. The trick was to keep his mind as occupied as possible with tasks that required concentration — so as not to think about the one thing he really didn't want to think about — but nothing so complicated that it felt like he was working.

So Luke dug some trenches for better drainage in the garden and he rebuilt a trellis for the climbing rose and he read two novels cover to cover.

He tried to not think about that one thing.

Except it was impossible.

For a couple of months now, it sometimes felt like it was the only thing he was thinking about.

Who was with Sadie when she died?

The photographs that had come through the letter box of his front door in London two months ago were meant as a warning. He was sure of it.

Hana was less sure. She had suggested that someone

simply wanted to hurt him. But that was really beside the point.

Someone had hurt Sadie. Someone had caused her death.

Sadie would want him to find the person responsible.

This point was one that Hana agreed on.

'When you find them,' she said to Luke one evening, 'then what?'

'What would you do, Hana?'

They looked at each other with an understanding that they wouldn't say the answer out loud.

Two

The ten o'clock news was often a good distraction and Luke had it on in the background as he was searching on his laptop for burlap covers for various plants in his garden. The lead story made him stop what he was doing and his head snapped up to stare at the screen. He fumbled with the remote to increase the volume.

A shooting at a restaurant in central London.

Luke peered at the television, trying to make out exactly where this had occurred. The news anchor stated that it was Bloomsbury and Luke swore under his breath.

Shootings were extremely rare, especially in central London. If he wasn't on a holiday, he would have been called to this scene with his level of seniority. There were no further details except that two people had been hurt.

Luke reached for his mobile and his first instinct was to call Hana. He suddenly realized that she wasn't reachable, so he called the person who was always next on his list.

It only rang once before Laura Rowdy answered.

'You're not working.'

Luke smiled. He should have known this is how she was going to answer the call.

'Right. But do you want to give me the details?'

'Holiday, Luke. Holiday. Do you even know what that means?'

'You know I'm just going to keep calling.'

There was a pause on the line while Rowdy considered this. He was absolutely right.

'A man, 40 years old, deceased at the scene. We have ID'd him. It looks like he was on a date with a woman. She has lost consciousness but is expected to survive. Currently in surgery so we haven't spoken to her yet.'

'Suspect?'

'Canvassing happening now and we're taking witness statements. CCTV will take a little while. We have DS Sharma on it here.'

'How much of the scene has been cordoned off?' Luke asked.

'A hell of a lot, Luke. This happened in Bloomsbury. We've shut everything off up to Euston Road, including Russell Square.'

'Good. Who's leading?'

Again, Rowdy paused.

'O'Donnell is leading.'

'I should come back,' Luke said immediately.

Before Luke could continue his thought, Rowdy jumped in to list off all of the various reasons that he should remain at the cottage, and the last reason being that he would inevitably be taking a look at everything on this particular case as soon as he returned in a few days time, Luke reluctantly agreed.

'I guess you haven't heard from Hana?' Rowdy asked.

Luke bit his lip slightly in an effort to not make a joke about Hana's whereabouts at the moment.

'Uh no, I'm not sure that I'll be hearing from her. I think that's rather beside the point for where she is right now.'

'Right,' said Rowdy. 'Well, at least she's sticking it out.'

'But can you imagine?'

'No,' Rowdy replied. 'I really cannot.'

———

As convincing as Rowdy was when she and Luke spoke, Luke had a fitful night's sleep. He couldn't get comfortable, he was slightly too hot, and he couldn't stop thinking about the rarity of a shooting in central London. It couldn't be random. That almost never happened. Why were these people targeted?

Rowdy had promised to text him when the woman had stabilized and Luke found himself waking every hour or so to check his phone. Finally at around six o'clock in the morning, the text from Rowdy was there. The woman was out of surgery and resting comfortably. She still had yet to be questioned.

A morning of wandering around the cottage made Luke feel even more restless. Determined to not pack in his so-called holiday and head back to London — he didn't want to give Rowdy the satisfaction somehow — he decided to head into Nailsworth to his favourite lunch spot. If he couldn't sit still at home, he may as well go somewhere he wanted to sit, and that was at Williams.

Driving towards the town, Luke decided he had better ring ahead to make sure he could get a table. Williams was a popular spot and he had gotten out of the habit of lunch there since Sadie had died. It was their usual Saturday spot and one of the places he could still stomach going to by himself. His stomach was, in fact, rumbling as he sped past the fields of sheep that dotted the rolling hills of Gloucestershire.

He hated using the hands-free system in his car but figured

the last thing he needed was to be pulled over for driving while talking on his mobile. It was Hana who had set the system up for him, muttering about his tendency towards being a Luddite as she did it.

His table confirmed, Luke drove on towards Nailsworth and found a parking spot just outside the restaurant. The little brass bell affixed to the top of the door jingled as Luke opened it, a detail that he loved. That Sadie had loved.

The first time they had walked into the restaurant, no booking in hand, feeling famished after looking at Bluffs Cottage, she had fallen in love with it. It had the charming small town atmosphere, and the friendly service to match. There were only eight tables at the back of the main floor of the building, the walls around them adorned with little framed paintings of crabs and lobsters and large fish of varying varieties that bordered on kitsch, but somehow were charming in Williams. In order to get to the restaurant, you had to walk through their deli, which took up the entire front half of the floor. The fresh seafood was glorious, but what caught Sadie's eye was the vast arrangement of delicacies for sale that would be found in the very best big city specialist food markets. A dozen different varieties of chilli paste, jars of pickles — all different colours and shapes and marinating with coriander seed or dill or rosemary. Sardines, anchovies, pâtés, chutneys, mustards. Before they had even sat down at their table on their very first visit, the condiments alone had won Sadie's heart. God, he missed his wife.

'Luke. Good to see you.'

Helen was a warm woman in her sixties, always smiling, always put her hand on your back while showing you to your table.

'Hi, Helen. How are you?'

'Same as always,' Helen said. 'Happy to see you, happy to feed you.'

Luke followed Helen through the deli towards his usual table in the corner of the restaurant. As she had done every time since Luke returned to Williams since Sadie had died, Helen hesitated slightly and waited for Luke to sit down before placing the menu in front of him. She did not want to assume that Luke would sit where he usually did, now opposite an empty chair where his wife used to be. It was a moment of respect, as if to say to Luke: I know she is not here, and I am sorry.

'Thanks, Helen,' said Luke. 'I appreciate that you still bring me this menu, but I'll have the usual, please. And a sparkling water.'

'No glass of wine today?'

'Not today.' Luke shook his head.

Either Helen hadn't noticed that since Sadie died he had never ordered a glass of wine in her restaurant, or she was being polite by not pointing this out. He was able to come to the restaurant and have his crab salad with a side of fries, but if he ordered a glass of wine as he used to do when he dined here with his wife, Luke worried that his sadness would overwhelm him.

As Helen nodded and walked off to put in his order, Luke made a mental note to himself to bring this up with his therapist. And then he chuckled to himself. How Sadie would love that he was making a list of things to discuss with his therapist about how he missed her.

Luke put the copy of the Times that he had brought with him on the table and unfolded it. The shooting in Bloomsbury was on the front page — not the headline news which was reserved for the latest in the Middle East conflict, but it was the second largest news story.

He was scanning the article when his mobile rang. Quickly putting it on silent so as not to be the asshole taking a call in a restaurant, he glanced at the screen. The name that flashed up surprised him.

Henry MacAskill.

Luke had last seen Henry a few weeks ago when he had used his journalist sleuthing to assist the Serious Crime Unit on the Grace Feist murder case and then the kidnapping of Poppy Travis. He was friendly with Henry and they met for a beer or two every couple of months, but this phone call was a little early to set something like that up. Something told Luke to answer it.

'Henry. Would you hold on just a second?'

'Sure.'

Luke stood up and signalled to Helen that he would be right back, and then eased himself through the glass door to the patio, all of its tables and chairs stacked in a corner now that it was the beginning of December.

'Sorry. I just needed to step outside. How are you, Henry?'

'Good. I hope I didn't catch you at a bad time. O'Donnell on your case over there?'

'I'm in Gloucestershire, actually,' Luke replied. 'A few days off.'

'Oh Christ. Sorry Luke. I didn't mean to bother you. Thought you'd be in the office with what happened last night.'

Luke didn't want to hear that. He was beginning to regret taking this mini holiday.

'Look, I'll be brief then,' Henry continued. 'It may be absolutely nothing, but I wanted to run something by you. I've had a letter here at the paper and I wonder if it is related to last night's shooting.'

'What does it say?' Luke turned to look back inside the restaurant. His crab salad was sitting on the table and he was torn between getting off this call and satisfying his hunger and hearing Henry out.

'It could be nothing. I'm really not sure. That's why I'm

calling you instead of speaking to the Met directly. I figure that you guys have enough going on over there. But if it's something...' Henry's voice trailed off.

'You're going to have to give me a bit more here, Henry.'

'It's a single piece of paper and typed on it is a little rhyme.'

'A rhyme?'

'I know. A little four line rhyme about two people being shot.'

'And it was addressed specifically to you?'

'It was,' Henry replied.

'Are there specific details on the note?'

'No. Look, cranks write in all the time about crimes, especially something high profile like this. We get them all the time. But the thing is, they usually come by email and this one didn't. And...in order to arrive at the paper in this morning's post, it had to have been posted before the shooting last night happened.'

Luke thought about this for a moment. A coincidence? Maybe. But maybe not.

'Okay,' Luke said. 'Maybe it's worth running this one over to the station. I can let Rowdy know that you'll stop by.'

'Is Hana around? I could meet her to pass it over. Might be easier, and a little less attention paid if this really is nothing, if you know what I mean.'

'Hana's also away at the moment.'

'Ah. Right. Listen, Luke, while I have you — did Hana mention anything about our breakfast?'

Luke wasn't sure what Henry was talking about, and tried to think back to when he and Henry had last had breakfast together. He couldn't remember that happening for quite a long time, or come to think of it, happening ever.

'I'm sorry, Henry. What breakfast?'

'A few weeks ago when I was helping you on the Grace

Feist case. Hana and I met briefly for breakfast. Well, she came into the cafe and I was there. She joined me.'

'No, she didn't mention it,' Luke said, his mind beginning to race.

'Right. Well, we had begun to chat about your wife and the circumstances there.'

Luke looked inside the restaurant again, this time knowing that he would be getting his crab salad to go.

'Henry?' was all Luke could get out of his mouth. 'I'm not following.'

'When are you back in London? Let's have a beer.'

Luke was already walking back into the restaurant, the rudeness of his mobile phone still attached to his ear no longer of any concern to him. He raised his eyebrows at Helen, who didn't quite understand what he was after, but some charade-like hand signals from Luke as he gestured towards his salad and then his car parked out front seemed to do the trick. Helen began packing his lunch and he finished his call with Henry.

'See you in a few hours,' Luke said as he finally hung up the phone and then apologized to Helen. Grateful he hadn't ordered a glass of wine, Luke hopped in his car and pulled away from the restaurant, wondering why he kept getting phone calls that altered the shape of his life.

THREE

Luke wolfed down the crab salad standing up at the kitchen counter in the cottage. There was no point in letting something this delicious go to waste. He looked around the cottage figuring out what needed to be done before he left. Stack the rest of the firewood, empty the refrigerator, take out the recycling, lower the thermostat.

And there was one more thing to do. Except he couldn't decide whether he should do it or not.

Luke chucked the salad container in the recycling box and rinsed the fork under the kitchen tap before tossing it into the dishwasher for the next visit. He hated being indecisive. It was a personality trait that he didn't usually possess, but the past few months had made him second guess a lot of things.

The question at hand today was: pick up Hana on the way back to London? Or not?

He had been treading a bit gingerly around Hana since she was released from hospital after being briefly kidnapped by Grace Feist's killers. This was something he was unused to doing. One of the things he loved about Hana was how straightforward she was. There was never any hidden meaning to the things she said. When she said she was going to do something, she did it. Apart from her tendency to wilt a bit when she was hungry — she was quickly revived. Never particularly moody, never unnecessarily irritated, always able to offer a joke in a situation that desperately needed it, Hana was the ideal partner. And the perfect friend.

When Sadie and Hana had begun to form their own friendship, Luke couldn't have been more delighted. There had been an evening a few years earlier that Sadie had come home a little tipsier than usual after what was supposed to be "a quick one" with Hana after work.

'You must never have another partner on the unit,' Sadie said, pouring herself a large glass of water as she swayed just slightly in the kitchen.

Luke tried not to laugh.

'What do you mean?'

'I mean,' Sadie said. 'I love her. I trust her. And I don't want anyone else working with you.'

'You mean, you trust me around her?' Luke offered, with a grin.

Sadie had shoved Luke gently when he said that, knowing that there wasn't that kind of trust issue in their marriage.

'She's special, Luke. I'm so glad I met her.'

Luke had poured himself a glass of water and the two of them had gone up to the bedroom. There hadn't been anything else to say at that point. He hadn't thought of Hana being particularly special at the time, but he understood what his wife meant. Sadie had being trying to say that she was the kind of person who made the mood improve just by being there. For Sadie, she experienced this as an emotional connection. Luke experienced this every day at work. Hana could ease the tension of a difficult situation, which was basically every single case they worked on. She wasn't necessarily the kind of person you instantly gravitated towards, but she was the person you didn't know you needed until you did.

After Sadie died, Luke felt this acutely. He needed Hana and this slight shift in their dynamic filtered through to the decision he was trying to make right now, standing in his kitchen in Bluffs Cottage.

Did Luke interrupt her week away to fill her in on what was happening in London? She would want to know and she would want to be involved, just as Luke did — that was a given. But why did Hana not mention she had seen Henry MacAskill? And what on earth had he said to her about Sadie's death?

To interrupt Hana's holiday for the first reason was one thing, but the second? He wasn't sure how well that would go down. And he had to factor in what Hana was doing on her holiday. When O'Donnell had instructed that they both take some time off, Hana had said she was heading away with a friend for the week. Luke knew of this friend, but had never met her and he assumed that they'd be heading to Paris, or Berlin, or somewhere very festive at the beginning of December, like Strasbourg. Hana was a sucker for a Christmas market and to hop on the Eurostar to the continent for a few days of shopping and mulled wine before Christmas was something she often did.

But that's not where Hana was right now.

Luke had thought he had heard incorrectly when she corrected him and said where she and her friend were heading.

'I'm sorry, you're going where?'

'Oxfordshire.'

'Yes, I got that part,' said Luke. 'But to where exactly?'

'A silent retreat.'

The pause where Luke wondered what to say, and tried to get his head around the fact that Hana was doing something so out of character, could have been taken as a comment on her destination, except he really was simply bewildered.

'A silent retreat,' he finally said.

'Yes. For five days.'

'You won't speak for five days.'

'Yes.'

At this point, he couldn't help himself.

'Are you serious?' Luke asked.

'I knew you were going to do this,' Hana replied with an audible sigh.

Luke held up his hands in mock surrender.

'I'm not doing anything,' he protested. 'I'm just trying to understand. I mean, Hana...'

'Look,' she said, clearly not wanting to discuss this with him. 'My friend was booked to go and she asked if I wanted to come with her. We got this time off out of nowhere and I just thought why not. It might be good for me right now.'

It was this last comment that stopped Luke from saying anything else that could be taken as flippant. He thought about what his wife would have said in this moment. Sadie would have smiled and said *good for you. It sounds really interesting. Tell me everything when you get back. Maybe I should do this!*

So Luke smiled and asked when she would be back and left it at that.

But now what to do? He could picture Hana's face when she arrived back in London after being sequestered away with no access to the outside world and discovered that Luke had rushed back to London from his break to deal with a serious shooting in Bloomsbury. She would be angry, but maybe she needed this time away? Maybe she didn't want to feel, for once, that she needed to be there for a particular incident and for the Serious Crime Unit and for her partner.

Luke finished his tasks and locked up the cottage. Sitting

in the front seat of his car, he did one more thing before pressing the ignition button. He had previously done an internet search for the retreat centre out of nothing more than curiosity. It had looked sort of spa-like in its sparseness and neutral decor, but the daily schedule looked painful. The sessions were called things like Connecting Through Quiet, Struggle with Self-Inquiry and Breathe Through Discomfort. But the item that caught Luke's eye and he simply could not imagine Hana dealing with was the phrase vegetarian menu.

Luke brought the website up again on his phone and pressed the call button. After a moment, a receptionist picked up but he was not allowed to be put through to Hana. Luke was invited to leave a message but was told that Hana would not receive it until the retreat had concluded.

'What if there is an emergency?'

'Is this an emergency? Hana has listed you as a close contact that we may disrupt her retreat for if there is an emergency,' the receptionist said.

Luke was touched by this and told the woman that this was not an emergency.

With the decision made, Luke pulled away from Bluffs Cottage and headed towards London. There was no need to rush as he wasn't meeting Henry until six thirty that evening and Luke enjoyed the first part of the drive, which went through several little villages, garlands and Christmas lights adorning doorways and lampposts.

Whether or not Henry was right about the anonymous note sent to him at the paper, Luke wasn't sure. He would quietly have a colleague run the note through forensics just in case, but it was Henry's mention of Sadie's death and speaking to Hana about it a few weeks ago that was the detail from the conversation that was lodged in him, almost like a splinter.

Why did he want to see Luke now? What was this all about?

As Luke approached the last junction before the M40 motorway, he slowed the car and looked at the sign that pointed left for London and right for Oxford.

Shit, he muttered under his breath and pushed the indicator level up with his index finger.

Four

L uke wasn't quite sure how to go about this.

He had pulled into the retreat centre's car park and stared at the front door. Feeling slightly too awkward about barging through it, especially having spoken to the receptionist only one hour earlier, he sat there debating what to do.

It was pretty quiet. Of course it was.

There didn't seem to be anyone around, so Luke figured he could walk around the building and get a sense of his next move.

The car door slammed behind him as he pushed it closed and Luke flinched. He stood still, as if he was a thief trying not to be seen in a motion detecting beam of a security light.

This is ridiculous, Luke thought, and began striding towards the end of the building, where he could see an expansive garden sitting to its right. The sound of his footsteps in the gravel of the car park seemed extra loud.

As he rounded the corner, he looked through the slightly foggy windows of the room and could see about ten people sitting in a semi-circle on the ground. There were pillar candles alight in the centre of the room that the group was facing. Luke realized that he could be seen through the window and suddenly felt very exposed and very aware he shouldn't be standing there staring in at a bunch of people who were supposed to be meditating. He could feel half a dozen pairs of eyes moving to focus on him. As he was about to get the hell out of sight, he caught one pair of eyes in particular.

It was the unmistakable stare of Hana Sawatsky.

Luke stood even more still than he had been before and watched Hana purse her lips and very slowly shake her head back and forth. Luke raised his hands up, palms toward the sky in the best apology he could muster in this bizarre situation. Then he pointed towards the car park and slinked away out of eyesight of the group.

Uh oh.

Luke stood next to his car, like a teenager who knew he was about to be told off for something that he also knew he should not have done. It was cold and just beginning to rain, that kind of winter rain that could be sleet and chilled to the bone.

The front door to the retreat centre whipped open and Hana stood just inside the entrance, pulling a cardigan around her to protect from the rush of cold air that must have just slammed into her. She gestured at him.

'I'm sorry...are you allowed to talk?' Luke started.

'Jesus,' Hana muttered under her breath and she disappeared inside the building, before returning with a pair of boots that she shoved her feet into and then stepped outside.

'What the hell are you doing here?'

'Hana, I'm sorry to intrude. I really am. It's just that I'm heading back into London and I was passing by,' Luke said.

'Are you kidding me?'

'Okay. Right. The point,' Luke continued. 'There has been a serious shooting in Bloomsbury. One dead, one injured and I'm heading back to the office. I thought you would want to know. But I'm sorry to interrupt your holiday. I shouldn't have bothered you.'

Luke turned to walk back to the driver's side of the car and then stopped short.

'One more thing,' he said. 'I'm meeting Henry Macaskill tonight. He said that you two spoke about Sadie a few weeks ago.'

At this comment, Hana looked down at her feet and pulled the cardigan tighter around her shoulders.

'Give me five minutes,' she said. 'I need to tell my friend I'm leaving.'

'Hana, you don't need to come back. Why don't you stay and finish the retreat? I can come back and collect you when it's finished.'

'Well I've opened my mouth now, haven't I?' Hana said. 'And besides, I am absolutely bloody starving.'

They were back on the road less than five minutes later.

'That didn't take long,' said Luke.

'I didn't exactly bring much. It's not like there were going to be great nights out here.'

Luke didn't say anything and they drove in silence for a couple of minutes until Hana told him to turn left at the next exit off the motorway.

'Why?' Luke asked.

'Because I see a sign for burgers. Honestly, if I don't eat something substantial soon I may expire.'

Luke pulled off the road and the two detectives settled into a diner that seemed to punch above its weight as a restaurant attached to a petrol station. It was busy and full of lorry drivers who had pulled off the motorway with the same idea. If it was popular with them, then the food had to be pretty good.

Luke filled Hana in on everything he knew.

'It was 7:40pm and a couple was having a drink at the Twelve Cases Wine Bar on Shutter Street in Bloomsbury. It's a quiet little road that is right next to the British Museum and has shops and restaurants on one side and a couple of offices and houses on the other. It's terraced on both sides, so no lanes or other exits,' Luke said.

'It is pedestrian only?'

'No,' replied Luke. 'But when I last spoke to Rowdy, she said that Sharma hadn't pulled up any useful CCTV yet. The second you get off that street, you're in the crush of the British Museum and Russell Square. No one is going to stand out there.'

'Someone with a gun certainly would,' said Hana. 'Ballistics?'

'I haven't got that far.'

Their food arrived and Luke watched Hana's burger being placed in front of her, as well as a bowl of fries, a Caesar salad and a side of onion rings.

'Are we sharing these?' the server asked, the plates hovering above the table as she waited to be instructed as to where to put them.

'Somehow I doubt that,' said Luke, and gestured to Hana, who had already taken a large bite of her burger.

'Could I have some mayo please?' she asked, her mouth full.

'Did they feed you at all in there?' Luke asked.

Hana shook her head and wiped her mouth with her napkin.

'And suspects? Anything at all?'

Luke felt like he was cheating on the crab salad from Williams as he bit into his turkey club sandwich.

'I doubt it. Rowdy would have called me,' he said. 'I'll check in with her before I meet with Henry tonight.'

'And how did this come about?' Hana asked.

'He called this morning. I really thought I'd stay at the cottage and try to relax for the rest of this week — let O'Donnell handle the shooting — but Henry's call rather changed everything.'

'In what way?'

'He said he received an anonymous note at the paper, which may or may not have been sent by the shooter. He didn't want to create a fuss if it was nothing, so I said I'd meet him and check it out. I'll run it through forensics, just in case.'

Hana didn't say anything, as if waiting for Luke to continue to the question she knew was coming.

'And he said he spoke to you a few weeks ago about Sadie. I was a bit taken aback. You didn't mention this to me,' Luke said.

'No,' Hana said, actually putting down the huge onion ring in her hand. 'I'm sorry that I didn't say anything, Luke. But...' Hana trailed off.

'What is it?'

'It's nothing, really. It's just...I was kidnapped right after I saw Henry and it wasn't exactly top of mind when I was in the hospital afterwards. And then I came back to work and I thought we just needed to put our heads down and not be distracted by anything. I was going to do some digging myself before I said anything to you.'

'What the hell did he say, Hana?'

Hana pushed her plate away from her.

'That's the thing. He didn't really say anything at all. Henry asked what I knew about Sadie's death.'

'What you knew?'

'Yes, I know,' said Hana. 'It's a little weird. That's all he said. He asked what I knew about her death.'

Luke was confused. Why would Henry MacAskill be

asking Hana about Sadie? Why did he ask him just hours ago if he knew the circumstances surrounding her death?

'What do you think this all means?' Luke asked her.

'No idea. But I bet you're about to find out.'

FIVE

Luke had dropped Hana off at her house in Shoreditch before heading home to drop off his own stuff and then heading out to meet Henry. It was partly convenience and partly wanting the universe to align in a way it had refused to do so for a long time that prompted his choice of venue for their chat.

The Draper's Arms was a short walk from Luke's house, and it was the setting of one of his first dates with Sadie — back when Luke's house was actually Sadie's house and he had yet to move into it.

Set slightly back from the street, cushioned by beautiful houses on each side, the pub was twinkling with soft white fairy lights and the temperature rose about twenty degrees the moment Luke stepped inside.

Luke was a bit early, and early on purpose, as he wanted a moment to collect himself before their dinner. He thought he may as well fortify himself too, so ordered a gin and tonic at the bar and leaned against it as he waited.

Did he want to remind himself of coming here with Sadie for the first time? He wasn't sure. Making a mental note of this question to ask his therapist when he next saw her, Luke marvelled at how his brain now worked like this.

When Hana had dragged him to see Dr. Nicky Bowman a few months after Sadie died, he had viewed the first meeting as a task he had to complete in order to get Hana off his back. He had no interest in speaking to a stranger about his wife, or engaging with her about the magnitude of what he had lost. And yet somehow over those first few weeks in therapy, he kept finding himself walking back to Nicky's house and sitting in her office and talking. And talking and talking. It had created a rhythm to his week, which had disappeared when Sadie died. No longer did he have a routine that included someone else but with his therapist, he found this again.

It was the way that Nicky paused before responding to him, carefully turning Luke's words over in her head. It was something that he tried to do when dealing with suspects — think about what they are really saying. What is hidden behind their words? And most crucially, what aren't they saying? Luke had to remind himself to pause and think before speaking to someone that had been dragged in front of him for questioning. But Nicky seemed to do this effortlessly and Luke had the feeling that she enjoyed this pause. She wanted to immerse herself in Luke's words and his world. It was enormously comforting.

So when Luke leaned against the bar in the Draper's Arms and wondered if he had chosen to meet Henry here because he perhaps needed to have Sadie as present as possible for him during this evening, he thought about what Nicky would say to him about it. He made a mental note to tell her this when he saw her next and he made another mental note to move up this session now that he was prematurely back in London.

Luke was curious about the note that arrived for Henry at the paper, but he was more anxious to hear what he had to say about his late wife. Why had he mentioned Sadie and the

circumstances of her death to Hana? No one but Luke and
Hana knew about the photographs that had been put through
the letterbox at Luke's home. The shocking photographs that
had taken their breath away. Sadie, just moments before her
death, not alone in her car as everyone assumed, but with
someone sitting behind her. Had this person held a weapon to
her throat? Had he been the one to grab the steering wheel and
force the car off the road and into the lake? Had he held her
head underwater until she drowned?

These were all of the things that kept Luke awake at night.
He tried to put them out of his mind, but it was impossible.

He hadn't told Dr. Nicky Bowman any of this yet.

How could he? What door would this open? One that he
wasn't quite willing or ready to walk through. He had told
himself, and had promised Hana, that when he had more
concrete detail about what had transpired that night, he would
tell his therapist.

And maybe tonight was the night the details would begin
to emerge. So Luke leaned against the bar at the Draper's
Arms, thinking about all of this but mostly missing his wife.

He was downing the last mouthful of his G&T when
Henry appeared. He nodded towards Luke and walked over to
him, his hand outstretched and the other hand unwrapping
his scarf that was tightly wound around his neck.

'Luke, thanks for meeting with me tonight. I'm sorry to
have pulled you away from the country and bring you back to
London.'

'Not at all,' Luke replied. 'I'm intrigued. And I'm starving.
Shall we?'

Henry nodded as he shrugged off his coat and the two men
were led to the upstairs dining room, one floor above the
bustling bar. They were seated at a quiet table in the corner,
for which Luke felt relieved, anxious to not have their conversation overheard.

Another drink and a sharing platter of charcuterie ordered, Luke asked to see the note.

Henry reached under the table and pulled up his shoulder bag. He unfastened the clip and reached in to extract a large plastic envelope, the kind that would hold a school essay. Henry passed it to Luke, who thanked him for placing the note in something clear and sterile and in something that zipped up.

The note was a plain, unlined sheet of paper that had been run through a printer. It had four typed lines on it. Luke read what was on the paper and looked up at Henry.

'A rhyme?'

Henry sipped his glass of wine.

'Yes, a goddamn rhyme,' he said. 'We get a lot of really weird post. It comes with the job and we take a look at everything that comes in. Some gets tossed right away, some gets filed, you know...just in case. But this one jumped out at me. You can see why.'

'Because it specifically mentions shooting.'

'Yes,' said Henry. 'And it had to have been posted before the shooting actually occurred.'

Luke looked at the rhyme again. It wasn't particularly interesting.

One, two.
I shot you.
Three, four.
Can't wait for more.

Luke turned the envelope over, as if something on the other side of the paper or the envelope might provide more of a clue.

'What is interesting is the envelope,' Luke said.

'Meaning?'

'Meaning that your name and the paper's address is handwritten. It's like he wasn't trying to be too careful. I'll have

Rowdy run this through forensics in case anything comes back on it. You never know.'

'Okay,' Henry replied. 'So not crazy that I wanted to show you this?'

Luke shook his head.

'No. The rhyme could be interpreted as a threat. Better safe than sorry.'

There was a pause in their conversation, which Luke tried to fill by sipping his wine very slowly.

'So you said you had breakfast with Hana?' he finally said.

'Yes, I did. A few weeks ago. How is she doing? Quite an ordeal she went through.'

'She's okay.'

'I've always liked her,' Henry said. 'Straightforward detective. No bullshit.'

Luke chuckled.

'You could say that again,' said Luke.

'What's her story?'

'What do you mean?' Luke asked.

'I mean...is she married? Single?'

'Are you serious, Henry? Didn't you get divorced, like, two minutes ago?' Luke laughed.

Henry shrugged as the charcuterie board was placed in front of them.

'Five years now,' he said. 'She's very pretty. But I don't want to complicate things.'

Luke picked up a large piece of prosciutto with his fingers and popped it into his mouth, quietly delighting in this slightly bizarre turn of conversation. Poor Henry, he thought to himself. Not a chance.

'I think, Henry,' Luke said, licking his finger, 'that you're not exactly what Hana is looking for. No offence.'

Henry smiled and nodded.

'Absolutely none taken. A guy has got to try.'

Luke suddenly felt more at ease with whatever Henry was going to say next. He liked Henry enormously, and he trusted him.

'When you called earlier today, you said that you had spoken to Hana about my wife?'

At the mention of Sadie, Henry put down his wine glass and slid the platter of meats and gherkins slightly away from the two men. He leaned towards Luke and looked directly at him. Henry's voice was softer and quieter when he spoke.

'I hope you will not be upset by anything I am about to say. Please understand that I've thought long and hard about saying anything at all. But if I was in your position - and I can only imagine how difficult this has been for you - I would want this to be said to me.'

What Luke wanted to say was, *Henry what on earth is it?* But Luke felt a lump in his throat that he felt might have prevented him from speaking, so instead he just nodded that he understood.

'It was a shock when Sadie died,' Henry said. 'You're well-liked at the Times, Luke, and everyone really felt for you.'

'Thanks,' Luke managed to whisper.

'But we are journalists first and foremost as well, Luke. And someone who works for me at the paper got ahold of the police report of your wife's accident. And that report made it onto my desk.'

Luke tried not to react, but it was hard to take this in. His rational brain understood that this happens all the time. Police reports are leaked to journalists — he wanted to throttle whoever had done it, but Henry had done nothing wrong here. The wife of a senior detective had been killed — a journalist would have had a look at it.

'Have you seen your wife's accident report, Luke?' Henry asked.

Luke had seen it. About a week after Sadie had died, he

had asked Rowdy to send it to him, which she obediently did although probably with hesitation. At the time, he hadn't wondered whether he should look at it or not. He wasn't even trying to understand what exactly had happened on road that evening when Sadie veered off it and into the lake. He had thought about how unlucky it was that she had gone off the road at exactly that spot, because that was the only section of road that ran along the lake. If the accident had happened anywhere else, she would likely have survived.

Luke knows now that this isn't exactly the case, but at the time, this twist of fate felt like agony.

When he looked at the report, he was probably still in shock. Luke wasn't looking for clues or for answers as to what exactly had happened. Instead he read the report as a kind of confirmation that she had been killed. Had Sadie died of a cancerous tumour, he would have looked at her MRI scan the same way — as proof that this is how she died.

'Yes,' Luke said to Henry. 'I looked at the accident report shortly after she died. Why?'

'Here's the thing,' Henry began to explain. 'I looked at the report twice. It was about a week apart. I looked at it when it landed on my desk the day after Sadie's accident and then I looked at it again maybe six or seven days later to check her date of birth. I wanted to be able to drop you a line around her birthday. I know that's always a difficult day when someone has passed away.'

Luke was beginning to get a sense of what Henry was about to say and he found himself pinching his thigh under the table in preparation for it.

'The reports were slightly different, Luke. I don't know what made me notice it, but I did.'

'What do you mean?' Luke whispered.

'The first report said that she was not wearing a seatbelt. The second one said that she was strapped into her seat. I don't know. It may be nothing, but it's a strange detail to be changed. I thought you should know.'

Luke stared at Henry across the table, suddenly feeling enormously grateful to him. This information made him feel less alone somehow and he thanked Henry for telling him this.

'Make of it what you will,' Henry said. 'But I wonder if perhaps someone working with you at the Met isn't a friend.'

'That list may be long,' Luke said.

Henry laughed, breaking the tension that had settled over the two of them.

'I know the feeling.'

Luke suddenly felt his mobile vibrating in his pocket and he apologized as he fished it out to turn it off. He saw that it was Rowdy calling at the exact moment Henry's mobile rang. Sheepishly, Henry also reached into his bag to find his phone and both men answered their calls at the same time.

As Rowdy spoke to Luke, he could see from the look on Henry's face that he was probably receiving the exact same piece of news.

Six

L iverpool Street Station on a Friday night at seven o'clock had to be one of the busiest places in London. Commuters waited in throngs for their trains back to the outskirts of the city, and then onwards to Essex and Suffolk and Norfolk. As the major train station closest to the City, you had bankers and lawyers letting off steam in all of the pubs and wine bars that encircled the station. And then just to the east of the station was Shoreditch, with its bustling night life that began early on a Friday evening. It was unlike the other, larger train stations in London due to these colliding elements but also because the station itself was small.

The ground level, had it been built today, would have been at least five or six times its existing size, in order to properly accommodate the modern day travel population for nineteen platforms. The upper level was sparse by comparison — a few shops and a small food store on one side and the top of the staircase that led up to the street level on the other. It sat at quite a height above the concourse below it, at the same level as the departure board.

When Luke arrived at the station, about twenty minutes

after the phone call that interrupted his dinner with Henry MacAskill, the station was empty and eerily quiet. He shivered as he entered the concourse from the side entrance, descending down the escalator that was the only thing still moving normally. The sirens that must have been screaming all the way to the station as multiple agencies were called to the scene by emergency services had been switched off. All trains had been cancelled and announcements paused. Every member of the public had been escorted out of the building. The only sound that Luke could hear was the crackle of police radios and the rhythmic clicking of the escalator slats hitting the bottom of the stairs and sliding back into place for their return journey in the underside of the moving walkway.

It was so unusual to see Liverpool Street Station like this that it only heightened Luke's sense of unease, which is a feeling he tried to shake off as he stepped onto the concourse. He needed a clear head and he needed to focus.

The body had fallen to the ground almost exactly in the middle of the concourse. He was face up, but his body twisted beneath him. His legs were to the side, slightly curled towards his torso as if he was sleeping and one arm was outstretched to the side, almost reaching away from him towards something.

The man's eyes were open and the side of his face was covered with blood which had come from his mouth. There was a lot of blood on the floor around his head that had been smeared across part of the concourse when emergency services had reached him. They had clearly reached him too late, although it was unlikely there had been any chance to save the poor soul at all.

The details became clearer to Luke as he approached the body, flashing his badge at a couple of uniformed officers who were protecting the scene.

The man looked to be about forty years old, dressed in a smart wool overcoat. It must have been unbuttoned when he fell, falling open to reveal silk lining and beautiful stitching. Luke motioned for an officer and asked for a pair of gloves. A pair was found and Luke pulled them on, the latex snapping against his wrists as he bent down to take a closer look at the body.

Luke pulled the overcoat back slightly and saw what he was looking for — the hand stitched label of the high-end tailor on Saville Row, and below that the initials C R in fine red thread. Underneath the coat, the man was wearing a smart navy blue suit, his tie slightly loosened. Luke guessed that the man had done this himself after a day at the office. The paramedic who reached him first would have seen what Luke was staring at. The side of the man's skull had been shattered by a bullet. There hadn't been any point in attempting to save his life.

Luke stood up and scanned the ground floor of the station. He had been right in the centre of the concourse in what must have been a frenetic moment at rush hour. Why had this particular man been shot?

It was at this moment that Luke heard the irritating pseudo-Irish lilt of Detective Superintendent Stephen O'Connell coming from behind him, barking orders at whoever would listen. Or at least be near enough to him to need to.

'Wiley. What are you doing here?'

'Sir,' Luke replied. 'I came back from my holiday a little bit early, and then I heard what happened this evening. I came straight here.'

O'Donnell looked annoyed, his first reaction always one that assumed the person he was dealing with was trying to usurp him or otherwise get in his way. But Luke could see the realization dawn across his face in real time — that he had someone to hand this unfolding disaster to, so he wasn't first in the firing line.

'Right. Your partner is speaking to witnesses on the top

level at the south entrance to the station. She's with the transport officer assigned to this station. I think he's in shock.'

'Understandable,' Luke said.

'This isn't good, Wiley. We don't know what we are dealing with here. If this is connected to the shooting last night in Bloomsbury, then we are absolutely fucked.'

'Understood, Sir.'

O'Donnell strode off to bark more orders and Luke looked up towards the south entrance of the station. He could just make out Hana speaking to a young man in a transport officer uniform who was sitting down, his head in his hands.

As he ascended the stairs towards them, he moved his hand towards the bannister and then stopped himself. A force of habit — he thought that he shouldn't touch it in case they were able to get prints off the metal. But then he realized that there would be thousands of prints on this hand rail and how enormous the task in front of them was going to be.

'Good evening,' Luke said as he reached the pair.

Hana excused herself from the young officer and moved Luke to the side so they could speak in private.

'Rowdy rang you right away, I see,' Luke said.

'You told her I was back?'

'I did. It wasn't my intention — we could have all used a bit more time off, but then this call came in. I figured you'd want to be here. Plus, you live just around the corner.'

'I didn't even have time to feed my cat,' Hana said. 'I came straight here when Rowdy called. The station had cleared out, but it was chaos outside.'

'It still is. The usual Friday night crowd, but also press. I was with Henry MacAskill when the call came in and he got the call at the exact same time.'

'Oh shit,' said Hana. 'Did you see the note that was posted to him at the paper?'

'I did. And the second Rowdy called about this shooting, I

told him to take it straight to the Met and hand it over to her. She knew to expect him and she is going to send it to forensics.'

'What do you think?'

'I didn't think much,' said Luke. 'But this evening rather changes things. How is the officer?' Luke nodded his head towards the young man who was staring into space.

'He's okay. I think he feels responsible, but there's no way he could have anticipated this.'

'And what is *this*, exactly?' Luke asked. 'I can see the victim, but what the hell happened?'

Hana walked back over to the officer and introduced him to DCI Wiley. The officer stood up and extended his hand. Luke shook it and clasped his other hand on the young man's shoulder as if to tell him that the events of the last hour were not his fault.

'Would you talk me through what you believe happened here tonight?' said Luke.

The officer moved about twenty feet to their right and stood next to the glass barrier that ran the length of this level of the upper concourse.

'We believe he was standing here,' the officer said.

'The victim?' Luke asked.

'No, Sir. The shooter. We have a witness who saw him standing here.'

Luke moved to stand next to the officer and looked over the balcony. It seemed about right from where the victim was lying. But to be so visible, standing here in front of the Friday evening crowds of commuters and party goers, to shoot someone below him?

Luke looked up and around him in a 360 degree motion.

'I know,' Hana said. 'Clever, isn't it?'

'What is?' asked the officer.

'No cameras,' Luke replied. 'It's a blind spot because of this pillar.'

Luke slapped his hand on the cement pillar, which was at least three feet in diameter and scaled to the top of the building. Moving around it to the other side, he could see the CCTV camera on the east side of the station angled right towards it.

'Surely the cameras outside the station will see him leaving though, Sir?' said the officer, although the inflection in his voice made this sound like an anxious question. The poor guy was worried he hadn't done his job properly.

But who would have expected this?

'I'm sure we'll get him on the cameras somewhere,' said Luke. 'Not to worry. And it wouldn't be a coincidence that he was standing here. He will have done some surveillance of the station beforehand. We have someone at the Serious Crime Unit who is a whiz with facial recognition. He'll find him.'

Hana agreed with Luke that Bobby Sharma was very good, but with two shootings in two days — if they were, indeed, related — she wondered how much time this would take him and how much time he was going to have.

'You said there were witnesses?' Luke asked.

Hana looked towards the entrance to the station. The police tape had set the cordon quite far back from where they were standing. It was one of the reasons that it was so quiet in the station — the murmur of the crowd had been kept away from the scene.

'Yes,' Hana said. 'It's those two women speaking to the other officer. I've taken their statement, but would you like to talk to them yourself?'

'What did they say?' Luke asked.

'He was white, about six feet tall, average build, no idea of age, with a black hoodie up around his head. He was wearing a long coat over the hoodie and after the shot, he just stood there. They didn't see him take the shot but when people started rushing over to the balcony, he looked over with everyone else and then as they started running away towards the street, he walked towards the exit very calmly. They didn't see where he went.'

'How did they know he was the one who took the shot?' Luke asked.

'They didn't at first. But this fine officer here,' Hana gestured towards the young lad who was actually shaking slightly, 'was up here immediately when he realized what had happened and asked for any witnesses. The two women came forward.'

'Well done,' Luke said to the officer, who looked relieved and managed a small smile.

'Shall I keep taking statements, Sir?'

Luke shook his head and relieved him of his duty. This wasn't Luke's remit in any way. He didn't even know who the officer reported to, except that this person, whoever he or she was, would be vastly outranked by Luke. He simply wanted to give the kid a break on what would have been his worst night on the job.

Hana and Luke walked back to the balcony and looked over to the concourse below. The coroner had arrived — it was Dr. Chung — probably called in from the very beginning of her weekend. They watched her, crouched next to the victim, staring at the body and taking it all in. She was precise at the best of times but would know that she needed to be extra precise tonight. Every little detail was going to count towards catching this killer.

Dr. Chung eased herself off the ground and moved aside, mouthing instructions to her colleague that Hana and Luke could not hear from where they were standing.

'What are you thinking?' Luke asked.

'I'm thinking that I have an extremely bad feeling about all of this.'

The two detectives stood in silence in the empty train station, observing the man splayed on the shiny white floor of the concourse that you never usually noticed when it was crowded with people. The blood that had poured from his head was still a brilliant crimson colour, and from their vantage point he looked like a wounded fallen angel plucked straight out of a Renaissance painting.

Luke wondered if the killer would have been pleased with his work of art.

SEVEN

At the station, Joy Lombardi was setting up the Incident Room, set at the back of the seventh floor of New Scotland Yard, the floor that was home to the Serious Crime Unit. The Incident Room hadn't been set up after the first shooting at the restaurant in Bloomsbury, even though she felt it should have been. Wasn't a random shooting in the heart of London, leaving one person dead, considered an incident of a magnitude that deserved its own dedicated space? But these decisions were not up to Lombardi, and there was a part of her that was relieved this was the case.

She loved being in the mix when a big case came their way — the buzz of the room they all worked in, the adrenaline she felt in her body, the piecing together of clues and figuring out a way forward — she loved it all. Her title was Analyst, which felt good to her. Maybe she would like it to be Senior Analyst at some point, the seniority of which would give her a bit more time off in the year and a better desk position when she wasn't working in the Incident Room, but apart from that, she was happy where she had landed. She knew that she was a little bit in awe of the detectives, especially of DS Sawatsky, who was only a few years older than her. Lombardi couldn't imagine being constantly out on the street investigating these crimes on the front line. They were hard enough to deal with from the relative comfort of the seventh floor of the Met. She knew she was much better suited to the grind of a case — the details that she liked to obsess over, the angles that perhaps no one had the time or inclination to follow. Lombardi was excellent at this layer of a case and it was the one place in her life that she felt completely competent and at ease. It's like this job had been her calling. If only she'd known this as a quiet, slightly awkward child who preferred her own company and the puzzle books she would lose hours in. It would have made for an easier childhood.

Lombardi moved the tables in the Incident Room to where they had been only weeks earlier, when Grace Feist had been found floating in the canal. She set up the white board at the front of the room and then went in search of the espresso machine. This was the most prized item at the Met, a force that could afford more than the two or three that floated around Scotland Yard, but they were like gold dust and hidden away in the corners of offices so not to be commandeered if at all possible.

The machine was found one floor below the Serious Crime Unit and handed over without much of a fuss when Lombardi pointed out that DCI Wiley would be setting up the task force to investigate not only the shooting from yesterday, but the one that was all over the news happening at this exact moment.

The first voice she heard as she waited for the team to assemble was O'Donnell's and Lombardi secretly prayed that he wouldn't be coming into the room before everyone else.

The door swung open and Stephen O'Donnell burst through it. So much for wishful thinking.

'No one else back from Liverpool Street Station yet?' he asked.

'Not yet, Sir. Just setting up here.'

'Thank you, Lombardi.'

Lombardi's head snapped up from what she was arranging at this comment. She wasn't aware that Superintendent O'Donnell had any idea what her name was. They stared at each other for a moment and then O'Donnell moved fully inside the Incident Room and shut the door behind him.

'Lombardi,' he began. 'I'd like you to do something for me.'

'What's that, Sir?'

'I'd like you to keep an eye on things.' O'Donnell paused. 'For me.'

Lombardi wasn't entirely sure what to say in response to this. She decided that the best course of action was to feign ignorance, not something she was used to doing.

'What do you mean exactly, Sir?'

'I mean keep watch on what is going on. How are Wiley and Sawatsky handling things, what exactly they're doing, who they are meeting with, that kind of thing.'

'I'm sure they will report all of that directly to you,' Lombardi replied.

'Yes,' O'Donnell said, in a tone that was more musing than a confirmation. 'But that's not exactly what I want. What I'm told by Wiley and Sawatsky may not be the entire story — and I want the entire story. If they are seeing someone that may or may not seem connected with this case, I want to be informed immediately. If they are going somewhere that seems unusual in the scope of these shootings, I want to know. Do we understand each other?'

Lombardi felt a chill in the room and tried to stop herself from shivering. She was incredibly uncomfortable and thinking quickly was one thing, but verbalizing something clever was another. Her brain scrambled to form words and she opened her mouth, waiting just a second, before answering her superior.

'This reporting into you. Why have you chosen me to do this, Sir?'

O'Donnell smirked at her and crossed his arms. He looked terribly pleased with himself, but to Lombardi's horror, she realized quickly by what he said next that he was actually pleased with *her*.

'Good question, Lombardi. Good question. I can see that you and I are the same. Or at least same wavelength, am I right? What is in this for you, you're thinking. How does this advance my career? How can I get...' O'Donnell paused, and his voice lowered sinisterly, 'to the top?'

Joy Lombardi's mouth opened, this time in protest, but no sound came out. She was stunned. And she wondered how the hell she suddenly found herself in this situation. All she was doing was hunting down the espresso machine and arranging tables in the formation that she knew Luke preferred and was waiting for him and for Hana to walk in the door so they could all get started. And now she was expected to be an informant?

She didn't want to wait for O'Donnell to have the chance to say another single word. She wanted him out of the room and she wanted him away from her. She would figure out what to do later.

'Understood, Sir.'

O'Donnell's smirk turned into a cruel smile, baring his teeth just slightly.

'I thought as much,' he said, before turning to leave, whipping the door open as if to catch anyone eavesdropping on the other side.

There was no one there.

Lombardi realized that she had been holding her breath.

The second O'Donnell left she inhaled deeply and busied herself with the espresso machine and coffee mugs. She opened the mini refrigerator that sat underneath the table she had arranged the mugs on and found it empty. She knew that Hana Sawatsky liked more milk than coffee in her coffee, so she grabbed her mobile and slipped it into her pocket before leaving in search of a carton she could pilfer from another kitchen in the building.

———

Stephen O'Donnell walked back to his office and shut the door behind him. He picked up the telephone receiver on his desk and began to dial the number, before thinking twice and gently placing the receiver back in its place. O'Donnell reached into his inside jacket pocket and pulled out his mobile phone and dialled the number again.

'Yes, it's me,' he said. 'I've heard tonight that DCI Wiley spoke to a journalist. Still gathering the details.'

There was a long pause as O'Donnell listened to the person on the other end of the line.

'Understood,' O'Donnell said. 'I'll make sure everything is handled.'

EIGHT

There was a decision to be made and Luke and Hana were discussing it with the senior police officers who had initially taken over the scene at Liverpool Street Station.

A next of kin needed to be contacted and the detectives were trying to figure out what to do.

The dead man lying on the concourse floor was Alexander Mathison, 44 years old. His wallet had been carefully pried from his trouser pocket and his driver's license showed a London address, a little north of the station. But what should have been a simple trip out to his home to inform anyone else who lived there was a little bit more complicated.

When the information had been relayed back to Rowdy, she had discovered that Alexander Mathison had a second address, a home in a Suffolk village. The small duffel bag that he had been carrying, which had fallen to the floor next to him when he was shot, confirmed that he was probably on his way there.

Hana had asked for some privacy when she bent down to unzip the bag. Luke knew her to do this, and found this small act of respect and compassion slightly strange, but a thoughtful gesture. To go through someone's belongings when they had just been murdered was something that could be done hastily and with recklessness when they were desperately searching for any piece of information that might help them catch the killer. But Hana always felt an enormous sense of responsibility with going through a victim's possessions.

As she gently pulled open the two sides of the duffel bag that she had unzipped, peering inside at its contents before touching anything, Hana thought about this man packing these particular items, having no idea that just a few hours later someone else would be touching them because he was dead.

Luke stood to the side watching her and pulled on a pair of latex gloves in case she suddenly wanted to pass anything his way. Hana had hoped to be able to carefully rummage through the items in order to see what everything was, but the bag was quite full and she would have to remove some clothing in order to properly see what was inside.

She removed a bulky jumper and carefully placed it across her thighs, so it wouldn't touch the ground. Now able to see a bit more clearly, she saw a pair of casual trainers, a laptop and laptop charger, a coffee thermos that was cool to the touch, a set of keys, and a folded, as yet unopened copy of today's Financial Times. This was the bag of a weekend commuter.

Hana had carefully placed the jumper on top of the bag, not yet putting it back inside in case they felt that the laptop needed to be opened there for any reason, before they took it back to the investigative eye of Bobby Sharma.

'What do you think?' Luke asked her.

'Does Rowdy see any listed dependents?'

'No.'

Hana took a breath while she considered the best course of action.

'I think we send a patrol car to both and see if there are lights on.'

'Okay,' Luke said, turning to the senior officer, who nodded and began to make the calls.

'Do you know anyone out in that part of Suffolk?' Hana asked.

'Doubt it,' Luke replied, hoping that there wouldn't be a tricky situation with different forces wanting to assert their authority over this situation. This was the last thing they needed when he already felt on the back foot in terms of their progress.

'What's your call here? If it's Suffolk, do you want to head out there?' Hana asked.

Luke shook his head.

'No, we're already wasting time. I want to get everything set up in the Incident Room and get going.'

'You don't have a good feeling about this,' Hana said, very matter of factly.

'Do you?'

Hana and Luke both looked towards the officer who still had his phone up to his ear, waiting to hear news on either house from the respective patrol cars that had been sent to check. The muffled sound of a mobile phone ringing was momentarily confusing, but both detectives suddenly realized where the sound was coming from.

Alexander Mathison must have had his mobile phone set to both an audible ringtone and the vibration function. One side of his suit jacket was moving slightly, and then paused briefly, and then moved again. It was as if he had started shallow breathing. A dead man come back to life.

'Jesus,' muttered Luke, as he reached inside the dead man's jacket and carefully removed his mobile phone.

Hana and Luke stared at the phone , which was lit up - the name Amelia Mathison emblazoned on the screen.

The two detectives were frozen in place, both thinking the same thing and knowing that the other was as well. There was the urge to answer the call, to get more information, to figure out who had shot this man in the middle of a busy Friday night rush hour.

But they couldn't answer.

On the other end of the phone was likely a woman who had no idea that her husband had just been murdered. Or even worse, it could be his child wondering where Daddy was.

Luke and Hana watched the phone ringing in his hand and then quiet again, the screen remaining lit for another moment before going dark.

'DCI Wiley,' the officer called over to him.

Luke stood up and approached the officer, still clutching Alexander Mathison's phone.

'No lights on at the London address. Looks like it's a shut up shop there. Patrol doesn't see any sign of anyone inside.'

'Thank you, officer.'

Staring at the phone screen, Luke looked like he was trying to calculate something in his head.

'What is it?' Hana asked.

'How long does the train take to get from London to Ipswich?'

The look on Hana's face could have been mistaken for irritation, but was really pure incredulity.

'Do I look like a walking timetable?' she said.

Sometimes Hana wasn't sure if this was Luke's brain working so much faster than everyone else's, or if he simply assumed that she had all of the information he needed right when he needed it. Either option was a nice one, except right now she would have laughed if the situation in front of them wasn't quite so serious.

'It's one hour on the fast service, Sir,' a helpful voice said from behind them, the officer who had summoned his patrol to check the house.

Luke looked up at the station departure board. The board still had the time and destination of the trains that had been due to leave when Alexander Mathison was shot. They all showed that they were cancelled — the activity of the usually bustling station on a Friday night, suspended, seemingly frozen in time forever on the board. The only thing that was functioning normally was the digital clock, ticking over every minute.

'How often do the trains go to Ipswich from this station?' Luke asked the officer.

'The fast ones are on the hour, and then it's an hour ten for the trains that leave on the half hour.

This time, Hana knew what Luke was about ask next, and she was searching for the answer on her phone, still crouched down next to the duffle bag, with Alexander Mathison's jumper balanced on her thighs.

'How far from Ipswich to the village where the second home is?' Luke asked.

'Not more than a twenty five minute drive, tops,' Hana replied.

Luke counted backwards in his head.

'He wasn't on the six o'clock because he wasn't shot until after that train would have left the station. He was going for the six thirty,' Luke said.

'But looks like he was late,' Hana offered. 'He wouldn't be at the house yet if he took the six thirty, so why the call?'

'We are jumping to conclusions, Hana,' Luke replied.

Hana took a deep breath and quietly agreed with him. They were absolutely jumping to conclusions and trying to fill in a gap where there may not even be one.

'If Amelia Mathison even is his wife, she could have been calling to ask him to pick something up on his way home from the station, or any other number of possible things and not necessarily about why he was late.'

Hana's instinct was to counter this theory. She couldn't help it, even though Luke was probably right. She wanted to keep going with this line of thought. She wanted to say: but if I wanted something picked up on the way home from the station and my husband didn't answer the call, I would send a text with instructions right away. As if to will this to happen, Hana stared at the phone in Luke's hand, which stayed silent.

Hana took one more look in the duffle bag, satisfied that they hadn't missed anything crucial for now and told Luke that they should head back to Scotland Yard. There was a huge amount to go through to get a good footing into this case and the Incident Room would be set up and waiting for them by now.

'One quick call into Rowdy and then let's go,' Luke said, carefully placing Alexander Mathison's mobile phone into an evidence bag and then keeping hold of it. It would go straight to Sharma when they returned to the Met.

Hana lifted up the bulky jumper to gently fold it before placing it back in the duffel bag and the sound of something hitting the concourse floor surprised her. She had just seen it with the corner of her eye — a square, rectangular cardboard box, slipping out of the jumper and dropping to the ground.

'Luke,' she said.

Pointing to the black box, she finally stood up and took a step back.

Luke beckoned to the officer next to him for another evidence bag.

Luke passed it to Hana, who carefully picked up the box and prised off the lid.

'Sneak peek?' she said to Luke, who couldn't help but join her to see what was inside.

It was a bracelet made of braided leather, its clasp a shiny silver.

'Jewelry for his wife? A Christmas present perhaps?' Luke said.

'I don't think so. This is a man's bracelet.'

'Hidden inside a jumper,' said Luke.

Hana placed the lid back on the box and carefully placed it in the evidence bag.

'There's a story here,' she said. 'Time to dig in.'

NINE

I t took the detectives another twenty minutes to get all of the evidence bagged and signed off on the removal of the body with Dr. Chung. By the time they were on the road and heading back to the station, Luke figured that the senior detective in the Suffolk county where they presumed Amelia Mathison — if that was, indeed, Alexander's wife — was waiting for him, would be arriving to deliver the terrible news.

Luke felt a mixture of emotions as he drove towards Scotland Yard, Hana sitting quietly next to him in the passenger seat. He would have preferred to deliver this news himself. It was always a dreadful moment. How difficult it was to speak words that were unspeakable. Your loved one is dead. Your person is gone. The life you knew is over.

It had taken Luke a long time — almost a full year — before he was able to describe how this felt for him when Hana had appeared out of nowhere on his doorstep to tell him that his wife was dead. When he first started seeing his therapist, he told Nicky that he couldn't really remember what had happened.

This was a lie.

He knew it to be a lie, but also occasionally questioned if he had, in fact, forgotten what had happened. Were they false memories? Had he filled in these painful gaps? He had only been forced to deliver this unspeakable news a couple of times since he had returned to work several months earlier and after his own experience, he now had a completely different understanding of what these poor souls were experiencing as the words came out of his mouth.

The uncertainty Luke felt when pressed by his therapist to talk about the moment Hana arrived at his house, and to try to talk about the moments afterwards, was created by something he could only describe as a kind of fracturing. To have your entire existence as you know it change in one single moment, and to realize that it had actually happened in a different moment earlier in the day that you were not present for, was a change so great and so fundamental that the human brain can't comprehend it.

Luke Wiley was one person before that moment and an entirely different person after it. How do you reconcile this within yourself?

'You talk about the moment,' Nicky had said to him when he uttered these words aloud.

'I don't see how this can help me.'

Nicky was always so still in her chair, only occasionally uncrossing her legs and then recrossing them the other way. She was a tall woman, and had Luke been examining her the way that he would someone relevant to a case, he would have thought that she was very comfortable in her own body and completely at ease with the conversation they were having. Luke wasn't used to someone sitting across from him in this kind of scenario being so at ease with themself.

Nicky had lifted her shoulders just slightly in a nonchalant shrug when he said this.

'You may be right. It may not help you at all. But why not try?'

And so Luke tried. He talked about how the words coming out of Hana's mouth were very clear and he understood what she was saying.

'Why did you immediately understand?' Nicky asked. 'Often people take a good few seconds — even minutes — to take in and comprehend this kind of shock.'

'I'm used to Hana delivering serious news. And her demeanour was not normal. I just understood right away.'

'What about her demeanour wasn't normal?'

Luke swallowed when he thought about it.

'She was in shock. I could tell. And she looked desperate.'

'Desperate?'

'Do you know what I mean?' Luke asked Nicky. 'That kind of desperation on someone's face? A sort of panic that invades the body against your will?'

'I do,' Nicky said softly. 'I know what you mean.'

'Would you like to tell me what happened next? What you remember happening?'

Luke found the words pouring out of him in a way he didn't expect. He had imagined telling Nicky all of this and thought that the story would be slow and painful to get out. The pain was there — his distress tipping him into tears that he was amazed to not be embarrassed by in front of Nicky. But the relief that he was able to get the words out in the first place overtook him and he told her everything that popped into his head, the images of what had happened flashing through his mind one after another after another.

Luke explained that the first thing he did, standing just inside his front door, Hana still outside on the doorstep, was pull his mobile phone out of his pocket and call Sadie.

'So you didn't believe what Hana was telling you?' Nicky asked.

'I'm not sure,' Luke said. 'It was instinct. But I don't think I was testing Hana or that I didn't believe her. It was something much more basic than that, I think.'

Nicky didn't say anything. She didn't prompt him to keep going, probably knowing that Luke didn't need any encouragement. The words were just going to come in their own time.

'It sounds strange — silly even,' Luke began. 'But I think I was calling Sadie to tell her.'

Nicky's mouth opened just slightly when Luke said this, but as if she thought twice about interrupting him, she closed it promptly and took a deep breath instead.

'She would always be the person I would call first if something happened. Something important, or something that was a shock. It was just instinct to call my wife.'

'But she didn't answer.'

'No,' Luke said. 'She didn't. And that's when I began to break down.'

'Do you want to tell me, or would you like to stop for a bit?' Nicky gently asked.

This part did remain a little bit muddled. Luke knew that he shouted out, but Hana told him later that he screamed, and that he did not stop until she wrapped her arms around him as tightly as she could and wrestled him further into the house, kicking the door shut behind her for privacy.

He remembered that they stood facing each other, not saying anything for a few moments. Luke realized that sweat had broken out on his lower back and even though it was a warm day, he suddenly felt very cold.

It was Hana who spoke first, calmly and slowly, understanding that they could do nothing except look at the information they had in front of them, just as they did together, every single day.

'I had a call into the unit. It was Gloucestershire Police.

Sadie's car went off the road at the A119 and into the lake just past Barnsley. No one saw it happen, but a member of the public called it in just before dusk.'

When he relayed this all to Nicky, Luke had paused for a moment to try to remember if Hana had uttered the words that they always said when they broke this news in the course of their job. Did Hana tell Luke that she was sorry? That she was so terribly, dreadfully sorry?

She had not.

And Luke explained this to his therapist. He explained that the loss was as great for Hana. Hana who Luke suspected made friends with ease, but not close ones. That Sadie and she had formed a bond. Her devastation was also enormous.

'Do you find comfort in this now?' Nicky asked him.

'What do you mean?' Luke asked.

Nicky uncrossed and crossed her legs, shifting slightly in her chair after sitting statue like as Luke had told her the story of the day of Sadie's death.

'I mean, is it comforting for you to understand that there is someone else who shares the depth of your grief?'

Luke answered without hesitation.

'Yes.'

———

As Luke and Hana drove from Liverpool Street Station towards Scotland Yard, he thought about these moments from a year and a half earlier. As if on cue, Hana asked a question, still staring out at the street in front of them.

'What are you thinking?'

'At this exact moment,' Luke said. 'I'm thinking about the notification in Suffolk.'

'You would have preferred to have done it,' Hana said.

'Actually, I was feeling a bit guilty for being relieved to not have to do it.'

Hana understood what Luke meant. Something that, although difficult, used to be routine and now held a different weight for them both. She felt the same relief.

Hana also had something else to ask. This was the first time the two detectives had found themselves alone, and they likely wouldn't be again for several hours.

'Did you talk to Henry MacAskill?'

'I did. Briefly. Would you believe that our phones rang at the exact same time about the shooting? The paper has excellent intel. I was almost embarrassed.'

'Luke,' Hana snapped. 'What the hell did he say?'

Luke didn't know why he was stalling. Perhaps he couldn't himself believe that what Henry said was true, and what it meant.

'Sorry,' Luke said. 'Yes, Henry wanted to speak to me about Sadie's death. The accident, specifically. By chance, he looked at the accident report twice. Once on the day after she died, and then again one week later.'

'And?'

'And the reports were slightly different. One detail had been changed. In the first report, Sadie was not wearing her seatbelt. In the second one, she was.'

Hana took a second to consider this.

'Henry thinks the report was changed,' Hana said.

'He does.'

'Sadie would have been wearing her seatbelt. Always,' Hana insisted.

'I know. She was a cautious driver.'

'She was.'

The two detectives seemed to be repeating and confirming the other's thoughts, as if the information they now had was too unbelievable to be true.

'There's only one reason that the police report would be changed,' Hana said.

'Well, two reasons,' Luke replied.

'If Sadie was actually not wearing her seatbelt when she was pulled out of the car, it means that she was alive and conscious when the car went into the water. She would have unbuckled it to try to escape.'

'That's reason one,' Luke said. 'Reason two is that somehow there is police involvement with her death. Why else would the report be changed?'

'Jesus,' Hana whispered.

Luke and Hana had previously wondered between them if Sadie's killer had been a cop, but the idea seemed too farfetched. Luke may have had disagreements with other members of the force, but to kill the wife of a DCI? What on earth could the reason be for such a heinous crime?

'Can I ask one more thing?' Hana said.

'I hate when you say that. Don't ask if you can ask a question. Just bloody well ask it.'

'Fine,' said Hana. 'Why would Henry MacAskill give you this information? What does he have to gain?'

'Gain?'

'Yeah,' said Hana. 'Do you really think he would doing this out of the goodness of his heart? Out of some moral obligation?'

The car had slowed for a traffic light and Luke seemed to press his foot into the brake pad extra slowly, as if he was trying to make a point. When the car had finally come to a stop, he turned to look straight at Hana.

'What are you saying, Hana?'

'I'm not saying anything. I just think we have to look at every angle of this. What does Henry have to gain by telling you that he saw two different police reports? And do you even believe him?'

'What the hell, Hana. Why on *earth* would Henry make this up? Put me through this grief all over again? He could only be trying to warn me about someone we work with.'

'Maybe,' Hana said. 'Look, you're probably right. But we also need to ask these kinds of questions. Sometimes I worry that you're not always seeing things as clearly as you need to. As we *both* need to. And that's understandable. This is Sadie. And we need to get it right.'

'You're not trusting me,' Luke said, his stomach fluttering as he said it. He hated feeling like he was at odds with his partner. They had gone through this earlier in the year and he loathed every minute of it.

'I do trust you,' Hana said, the tone of her voice suddenly much softer.

The traffic light changed from red to amber and to green and Luke released his foot from the brake and they set off again, only a few minutes away from their parking spot just off the Embankment.

'But you know what?' Hana continued. 'I'd trust you a whole lot more if you would finally tell Nicky about what has happened. You need to tell her, Luke. About the photos delivered to your house, about what Henry said to you, about what you think and how it's affecting you.'

Luke didn't reply as they turned the corner, the streetlights making slight shadows on the banks of the dark Thames, shimmering and black at this time of night. But he knew she was right.

TEN

The smell of slightly burnt espresso hit Luke and Hana as soon as they stepped off the lift onto the seventh floor of New Scotland Yard. It was approaching ten o'clock at night but the Serious Crime Unit was still bustling with staff on computers, logging phone calls, and gathering as much information about the events of the past two days as they could.

Luke didn't care for this kind of chaos. He wasn't the kind of person who thrived in it. He needed the information to be ordered and the details clear so the picture of what was happening could form in front of him. Luke knew that too much information was about to come barrelling at them as they entered the Incident Room, much of it unhelpful, and no one yet knowing what was crucial and what wasn't. He was bracing himself for the next hour.

Hana, on the other hand, could feel the adrenaline spike in her body as the buzz of the unit hit her when she walked down the corridor. She was lifted by this energy and she liked the frenetic pace of her colleagues. The more they could find for them, the more they had to work with and she could spend hours happily sorting through the details until she found what they didn't know they were looking for. It was the kind of chaos that could bring a lot of luck their way.

Both detectives could hear O'Donnell barking at someone in his office and they instinctively moved to the path of least resistance to get to the Incident Room, easing around desks and towards the side of the floor that did not run past his office. Luke could see that Laura Rowdy was also on the phone, standing up as she liked to do when life on the unit got busy, and he signalled to her that he'd like her to join them as soon as she was finished.

Luke and Hana paused just outside the Incident Room. They turned to look at each other as if to say: *here we go.* Hana turned the handle on the door and flung it open.

Three heads whipped towards them. Two they were expecting. One was a complete surprise.

'Parker!' said Luke.

'Sir.'

Officer Parker stepped forward to shake Luke's hand and then looked past him.

'DS Sawatsky. Hi. How are you feeling?' he said, a sheepish smile forming on his lips which he tried to hide by biting his lip. It was a poor disguise not missed by anyone in the room.

'What are you doing here, Parker?' Hana asked.

'Oh, you're speaking now are you?' said Rowdy, standing at the door.

This quip made Luke actually wince. Only Rowdy could get away with a comment like that.

'I called him,' said Rowdy.

'Could we perhaps speak about this later?' Hana said to her.

'Officer Parker not only saved your life,' Rowdy replied, 'but he was instrumental in cracking the case the last time we were all in here. I'm sure no one needs reminding of that. And it's all hands on deck. I made an executive decision.'

Luke chuckled. *Executive decision*. The only person he would have dared allow to go over his head like this would be Laura Rowdy — and everyone in the room knew that, too.

'Good to have you here, Parker,' Luke said. 'We'll see how everything goes and how much you can be spared from your usual role, but have a seat for now.'

'Rowdy, would you please bring us all up to speed? Sharma and Lombardi, please jump in should you think anything needs to be mentioned specifically. Hana and I have a bit of catching up to do here and we're already behind.'

Lombardi pulled a large notepad, the kind that lawyers tended to use, towards her and clicked the top of her pen to expose the nib. Luke smiled to himself, enjoying the old-school method of note taking, and one that he was partial to himself.

Rowdy grabbed a bottle of water from the table to the left of the door, twisted the cap open and took a big slug before standing in front of the room like a school headmistress.

Someone had already divided the board at the front of the room into three columns. On the left was Shooting 1, on the right was Shooting 2, and the column in the middle was blank. The feeling in the room was that these shootings were connected, although there was no evidence yet to support this theory.

'The first shooting occurred yesterday, Thursday evening at approximately seven o'clock,' Rowdy began. 'The location was a wine bar slash restaurant called The Twelve Cases. It's on the end of a block on Shutter Street, just around the corner from the British Museum. Two victims. 40 year old Trevor Alpine deceased at the scene. 36 year old Lisa Owens wounded and transported to hospital where she underwent surgery for a gunshot wound to the shoulder. She is conscious and is expected to be released from hospital over the next few days.'

'Lucky,' said Hana.

'Extremely,' Rowdy replied. 'There were three shots fired. The first went into the wall behind the diners, miraculously not hitting anyone. The second hit Trevor Alpine and the third hit Lisa Owens.'

'Ballistics come back yet?' Luke asked.

'Yes,' Rowdy picked up the pen and began to write as she kept talking. 'The weapon used was not a rifle as we first suspected.'

'What was the original theory from officers on the scene?' Luke asked, irritated that he had been in the Cotswolds at the cottage when this happened, and not first at the scene so he could have gotten a sense of it himself.

'A hunting rifle, something like a Remington or a Tikka, single barrel, accurate — the kind of gun used in deer stalking. It's quite a common gun.'

'But also accurate, right?' said Hana. 'If the shooter was only on the other side of the street, he wouldn't have needed three shots to hit two people.'

'Depends on the skill level, I suppose,' said Sharma from across the room.

'Okay,' Luke said. 'So ballistics came back with what?'

Rowdy wrote .22 LBR on the board.

'A long barrelled revolver?' said Hana. 'Shit.'

'What?' asked Luke.

It was Sharma who replied as Hana stared at the board.

'It's a pretty common gun that you need a Section 1 license for, but it's not as simple as tracking down a cartridge to a specific gun and then finding the owner. It's very hard to track and this gun is very commonly stolen.'

'I take it you've been searching already,' Luke said.

'Yes. No luck yet, Sir,' Sharma replied.

Luke looked over at Hana, who would have already known all of this from her military training, so he assumed that something else had just made her swear.

'You can fit a scope on this kind of long barrelled revolver,' Hana said. 'But even so, you'd have to be a pretty decent shot to hit your target.'

'Even if your target wasn't moving?' Luke asked.

'I'm due my firearm refresher next year, but even so, I wonder if I would so easily hit someone through a window and from across the street. In the dark.'

'But isn't this a good thing?' Lombardi piped up. 'Easier to track down a skilled shooter than some random gun aficionado?'

'We'd better hope so,' said Luke. 'Sharma, anything on CCTV?'

'There's nothing on that street except a camera on one of the shops next to the wine bar and that was disabled last month. None of the houses across the street have doorbell cameras, I'm afraid. We've put out a public request for dash cam footage around Russell Square for the two hours prior to the shooting and one hour post, but it's going to take awhile to go through it all, especially as we don't know what we're looking for yet.'

'Well, if we're lucky, we'll get a shot of someone strolling down the street with a long barrelled revolver sticking out of his jacket pocket. You never know,' Hana said.

The room was silent until Parker managed a conciliatory laugh that stuck in his throat slightly. He coughed and looked embarrassed.

'How many shots were fired tonight?' Rowdy asked.

'Initial report is just one,' Luke said. 'And it was loud. People scattered as soon as they realized what had happened, and that happened pretty quickly.'

'You're thinking it's the same guy,' said Hana.

'If he's that good of a shot, it may be. God help us,' Luke said.

The Incident Room remained quiet as they took this in. If the shootings were linked, and it was the same shooter, the city of London would begin to panic.

'Has next of kin been notified for the deceased last night?' Luke asked.

'Yes,' said Rowdy. 'Trevor Alpine's parents have been informed.'

'Where do they live?'

'Dorset. They have support officers with them, but I believe they are planning to travel to London tomorrow.'

'Okay. Do we have any sense of motive whatsoever?' asked Luke.

The room was silent once again.

'Well then we'd better go and speak to the one person who is still alive.'

ELEVEN

By the time they finished going through all of the details and getting the information up on the board, it was past midnight. Although hospital visiting hours didn't apply for the detectives, it seemed too disruptive to visit Lisa Owens at that time of night, so the detectives headed home to try to get some sleep.

It was a bit of a futile exercise for Luke. He fell off right away, experiencing that adrenaline crash that was so familiar to him when working on a case, but as if he had drunk too much wine during the evening, his body was wide awake by five o'clock in the morning. Once upon a time, he would have cursed the booze but at least happy at a fun night out, but this morning he only felt groggy and anxious.

He didn't even bother to fight his way back to sleep for another hour or so and the temperature in the house was slightly bracing. Even with the double glazing on the windows and the underfloor heating that Sadie had put into many of the rooms when she knocked the two houses together in Arlington Square and created this beautiful house, the fact remained that it was England and the house was inevitably cold in winter.

Luke pulled on the nearest pair of tracksuit bottoms and shoved his feet into a pair of wool lined moccasins that lived on the floor next to the bed and he rummaged in the laundry basket for his sweatshirt which he had tossed in there before leaving on his week away in the country. He sniffed the sleeve as he put it on and to his relief, it didn't need to be washed right away.

Turning the dial on the thermostat up slightly, he made his way downstairs and filled the kettle with water, switching it on and pulling a bag of coffee beans out of the freezer. As he prepared his morning brew with his usual fastidiousness, looking at the second hand on his watch which he hadn't remembered to take off before crawling into bed, he flicked the switch for the gas fireplace in the kitchen and it sprang to life. In another ten minutes, the kitchen would be toasty warm.

'Shit,' Luke muttered aloud, as he discovered that he didn't have any milk in the refrigerator. Sipping his coffee black, it was too hot and he scalded his tongue in the kind of way that he would be reminded about for the rest of the day.

'Shit!'

Luke opened the cutlery drawer where, for some bizarre reason that only made sense to his late wife but he kept the tradition alive, the remote control for the television was kept. He turned the tv on and increased the volume when the familiar theme tune for the first morning news chimed through the kitchen. Luke checked his watch again and saw that it was five thirty. At this time of the year, it wouldn't be properly light for at least two more hours.

The lead story was predictably about the shooting at Liverpool Street Station. It took Luke a moment, squinting at the reporter standing outside the station, to determine if this was footage from last night or was live. Only when she announced that the station would be reopening for all departing and arriving trains at six am did he understand that it was live. He couldn't help but marvel at this — a man was executed in the station twelve hours earlier and everything was back up and running again. Life continues on in the midst of tragedy, the rest of the world moving forward without a thought.

Luke looked for his phone so he could check his messages and cursed a third time that he had left it upstairs in the bedroom. Climbing the stairs he flicked on a couple of overhead lights to try to spur himself into the day and retrieved his mobile from the bedside table. As he went to head back downstairs, something made him stop by the bedroom closet. This sometimes happened, this pull towards his dead wife and the things she had left behind. Often he tried to ignore it, but this made him feel slightly guilty or that he was being silly for not taking the moment to think about her. How to explain this to someone who hadn't lost their person? He tried in therapy, perhaps to some avail, but the feeling still lingered.

Sadie had loved clothes. Fashion wasn't necessarily something she was too bothered with — instead she was the kind of person who had seven or eight grey blazers that all looked the same, but had unique differences and feel to her. So when she renovated the house, the closet attached to the bedroom was made an enormous size.

Luke had often found himself in the closet not to choose or fetch an item to put on, but to look at Sadie's clothes. To touch them. To run his hand down the blazer sleeves as if she was still inside the jacket, to smooth out a crease for her.

He thought that the task of sorting out her closet and disposing her clothes would be an agonizing one and he had waited a couple of months to do it. But finally the weight of her absence and how heavy it became every time he looked at the trousers and t-shirts and shoes became too much and Luke and Hana began to sort through everything. The task was enormously sad because of what it represented, but it wasn't as acutely painful as he thought it would be. Hana kept a few things and donated most of the rest. A few pieces were kept — ones that Luke could picture Sadie in the most often, or he knew that she loved. These remained hanging in the closet, next to his things, a small momento to make him feel as though she was still a part of his day.

The harder task had been to face the moment she was living in when she died — the items that reflected this like the novel on her bedside table, the watch she had chosen not to put on that day, the sudoku book she was working through. All of these things were placed in a couple of boxes and shoved into the corner of the closet on the floor. Luke still couldn't bear to open them and see what was inside.

His phone beeped in his hand and he looked down at the screen. He read the text message and shoved the phone back in his pocket.

———

Hana had not been home from the silent retreat for very long before Rowdy rang her to tell her about the shooting at Liverpool Street Station. When she finally returned close to one o'clock in the morning, she was exhausted. So much for the restorative process that had been promised at the retreat. Would she have felt differently if she had completed it and not been at the scene of a major incident in one of the busiest locations in London tonight?

She doubted it.

Hana's cat had curled himself into her small wheelie suitcase which she had just had time to open, but not yet unpack, before Rowdy's call had come in. Max, the large tabby, seemed to be indicating that she was not to go away again anytime soon. He opened his eyes briefly when she opened her front door and then locked it again behind her, stretched, and then went back to sleep.

She felt wired but was desperate to sleep. It was going to be a long day tomorrow. She checked the time on her microwave — it was already tomorrow.

Opening the bottom cupboard of her kitchen island, she pulled out a bottle of Oban whiskey and poured a small slug into a heavy bottomed glass and took it upstairs with her. Kicking off her shoes and peeling off the clothes she had been wearing since she hurriedly threw them on when Luke had arrived at the retreat centre, not wanting to travel back to London in yoga gear, she sipped her whiskey and crawled into bed.

This is not a good look, Hana thought to herself as she sat in the dark under her duvet, clutching her glass. She was usually very strict with herself about not staring at a screen before going to sleep, but tonight was an exception in so many ways.

The blue tinged light from her mobile illuminated her small bedroom and she scanned the news of the day. No new story was as gripping as the two shootings and she read the latest coverage in each of the major newspapers and network websites. Journalists liked to speculate and this always made their job infinitely harder. But the only mention of the two shootings was to say that there was at present no link between them. Hana scrolled down to the reader comments and took a quick look — there were a few mutterings about gangs and crime and the police not doing their job properly. For now, that would do. If the shootings were, in fact, connected, these news articles were not going to look like this for long.

When Hana next looked at her phone, it was almost six o'clock and she was amazed that she had slept for five hours. She was still propped up on her pillows, her neck aching but her glass of whiskey miraculously on the table next to the bed. She ran her tongue against her teeth and grimaced.

She eased herself out of bed and turned on the shower, twisting the temperature handle to make it as scalding as she knew she would be able to stand. As she waited for the water to heat and the steam slowly began to form in the bathroom, she thought about Henry MacAskill and the two differing police reports. She couldn't help but be suspicious — it was simply her nature. Or maybe her suspicion had nothing to do with Henry, but at the entire situation. She had been shattered by the photographs of Sadie in her last moments, delivered anonymously to Luke's house like a message from the devil himself.

She had not slept soundly since her first glimpse of them. How ridiculous to think that a week long retreat in silence would fix anything for her? She knew that Luke was not sleeping either. How could he?

The only thing she wanted, even before knowing who killed Sadie Wiley, was for Luke to have a clear head. They needed to do this together. They needed to be a team.

They only had each other.

Hana squeezed a large blob of toothpaste onto her toothbrush and stuck it in her mouth. Stepping into the steaming hot shower, she brushed her teeth and let the water pour over her head. She suddenly stopped what she was doing and stepped out of the shower. Rinsing her mouth, she walked back into the bedroom leaving a wet trail behind her. Hana picked up her phone and fired off a text message and threw her phone back onto the bed.

TWELVE

After Luke had responded to the text, he sent another one to Hana to tell her that he'd meet her at the hospital. One of Lisa Owen's lucky escapes on Thursday night was that she was shot in a wine bar just blocks away from one of London's major trauma centres.

At seven in the morning, the bus that Luke had jumped on at the end of the street that connected Arlington Square to Upper Street was quiet on a Saturday. It was still dark outside, the Christmas lights still twinkling in shop windows and the detritus from a festive Friday night out still littered the streets.

It had been awhile since Luke had been inside University College London Hospital, and not since he had been back at work. Wondering if the coffee cart that had a selection of different beans you could choose from — highly unusual to find in a hospital — was still towards the side of the lobby, Luke ventured into the towering building.

Standing next to the cart was Hana, clutching a large cup of something that would be so milky there was barely a point in drinking it.

'I didn't dare choose your bean,' she said.

'Smart thinking.'

Luke looked at the board and went with Eithiopian and a double espresso.

'Have you let anyone know we're here?' Luke asked.

Hana nodded.

'We are welcome to head up and speak to Lisa anytime. She is awake and has already been visited in morning rounds. She knows we are coming.'

'Great.'

Luke sipped the espresso from the little paper cup as they walked towards the lift. Hana had to stop herself from rolling her eyes at the doctors they joined, all holding giant coffees, as they made their way up to the third floor.

The nurse at the station saw the detectives coming and came out to greet them.

'She has already been questioned by officers yesterday and she found that exhausting. So as brief as possible please?' she instructed.

'Understood,' said Hana, as they followed the nurse down the hall to the patient's room and were left to it.

Luke knocked gently on the open door and the woman in the bed turned to face them.

'Hi,' she said, quietly.

'Lisa? Good morning. I'm DS Hana Sawatsky and this is my partner, DCI Luke Wiley. I'm sorry that we are bothering you so early in the morning, but can we speak to you for a little bit?'

'Yes, they told me you were coming.'

Hana nodded gratefully at her and Luke gently shut the door behind them so they could have some privacy. Luckily, the bed next to Lisa was empty.

Hospital beds have the habit of making their patient seem small. Lisa Owen looked fragile, her dark blonde hair hanging limply at the sides of her face. She had very pretty features which somehow were more striking than they probably were because of how pale she was. The side of her jaw was bruised and slightly swollen.

'Did that happen as you fell?' Hana said, pointing to her face. 'It looks painful.'

'Apparently not. The doctor said that it's likely my shoulder went up into my jaw when the bullet hit it. It's an involuntary movement or something.'

'You've been through a lot, and I'm sorry to have to ask you to go over things that you've already spoken to other officers about. We have taken over your case and want to make sure that we completely understand everything that happened,' Luke said.

'That's fine.'

'Can we get you anything before we start?' Hana asked.

'No, I'm okay.'

The calm, steady answers made Hana wonder if Lisa was still in shock. It wouldn't be unusual after a trauma such as this one. The body heals much more quickly than the brain.

'We understand from the initial report that you hadn't been in the wine bar for very long until you were shot?'

'I'd say it was about twenty minutes. We were still on our first glass of wine and some padron peppers had just been delivered to us. I remember that I was just about to pick one up when the glass splintered and we heard a bang. I didn't realize what the noise was at the time.'

'What do you remember about the twenty minutes?' Luke asked. 'Was there anyone already sitting where you were when you came in? Did anyone hold the door open for you when you entered? Did the staff say anything in particular to you? Did anyone stick out to you in the bar? Things like that.'

Lisa took a second to take in Luke's question and then asked one of her own.

'Do you think we were targeted?'

Luke and Hana looked at each other.

'Honestly, Lisa, we don't know yet,' Hana said.

'Do you have any reason to believe that someone would want to do this to you?' Luke asked.

'To me? Why me?'

Lisa shuffled in the bed, the anxiety visible on her face.

'What happened in those twenty minutes?' Luke gently prodded again.

At this point, Lisa began to cry. Her tears were silent, and slid slowly down her face and her breathing rasped in the staccato way that happens when someone is trying not to cry.

'I'm sorry,' Hana said, feeling immense sympathy for her. This poor woman who was just on a date and then shot in the middle of it for a reason they couldn't determine yet. The whole thing was awful.

'It's just,' Lisa stammered, 'it was a great twenty minutes. I hadn't seen Trevor for a few weeks. I thought he wasn't interested in me anymore and then I was so relieved when he called me. It was amazing to see him and he seemed thrilled to see me, too, and he apologized for not being in touch. I remember thinking how great everything was going and then...'

Lisa began to sob now and Hana instinctively reached out and touched the arm that wasn't bandaged and held in a sling.

'It's okay,' Hana said. 'Take your time.'

'I just don't understand why this has happened. He didn't deserve this. I think this is all my fault,' Lisa whispered between sobs, the words barely getting out of her mouth.

'What do you mean, Lisa?'

Both Hana and Luke stretched forward slightly, sensing that they were about to get more of the story now — the part of the story that they needed.

'I was late,' Lisa said. 'I was late on purpose, just hanging around waiting to go in the bar. It was so stupid. If I hadn't done that, we might not have been sitting there. This wouldn't have happened.'

'I don't quite understand,' Luke said. 'What do you mean that you were late on purpose?'

As Lisa explained why she was late and the entire psychological drama behind it, Hana could see from the quizzical look on Luke's face that he wasn't comprehending the various reasons Lisa had for making Trevor wait for her. She shot him a look as if to say: *I'll explain later*, and proceeded to coax a bit more of the story out of the poor woman.

'Lisa, where were you waiting? Were you by the wine bar?' Hana asked.

'Yes — just a block away. I was standing on Princely Court.'

'Where exactly?'

'Right on the corner — but Trevor couldn't see me where I was standing. I wasn't in view of the bar.'

'Did you see anyone around you while you were standing there? Did you speak to anyone or see anything unusual?'

Lisa shook her head.

'Do you really think someone was watching me?' she whispered.

'It's unlikely,' Luke said, trying to give her a reassuring smile. 'We are just covering everything as even the smallest detail can help. It's perfectly routine.'

'What about Trevor? What was he like? Can you tell us a little bit about him?' Hana prompted.

Lisa took a deep breath, her chest shuddering slightly as the tears subsided. She explained mostly what they already knew from the initial report. Forty years old. Lawyer. Lived alone in a flat close to London Bridge. Successful. Handsome.

'He really seemed to listen, you know? I'm not sure a lot of guys are like that. I know we had only been dating a few weeks, and god I am a little rusty at it, but I felt for sure on Thursday that there was a future. That we had a future together.'

'I'm so sorry,' Hana said.

Luke was quiet for a moment, taking in everything that Lisa was saying, trying to piece it all together in his mind. Only one thing stood out to him at this point in what was otherwise an uneventful, normal story about two people who were dating.

'You said that you didn't hear from Trevor for three weeks. Why was that?'

'We didn't really get into it,' Lisa replied. 'He apologized and said he felt bad that he hadn't called, but he was just distracted at work.'

'He didn't say anything beyond that?'

'No.'

Hana and Luke shot another quick look at each other across their patient. The next order of business was going to be figuring out exactly what Trevor Alpine had been up to for the past three weeks.

'We are probably going to be back with other questions, I'm afraid,' Luke said. 'But why don't we leave you to rest for now. We understand that you could be discharged as early as tomorrow.'

'Yes. But I'm not too sure about going home. I might be staying with my husband.'

Hana, who had been in the process of standing up and putting her coat on, suddenly froze in place, one arm inside the coat sleeve and the other hanging in mid-air.

'I'm sorry?' she said.

'Sorry,' Lisa said. 'My ex-husband. I know it sounds strange but even though we aren't married anymore, it's a familiar place to be. I don't want to be alone.'

'Right,' Luke said.

Lisa pointed with her free hand to the large bouquet of roses sitting on the table opposite them.

'He brought these,' she said. 'It's so funny, we hadn't be in touch for months — it wasn't a particularly friendly split — I start dating someone and think everything is moving forward, and then this. Not exactly how I pictured it.'

'It never is,' Luke said, looking at Hana one more time.

THIRTEEN

'It's the husband,' Hana said, as soon as soon as they walked out of the hospital, daylight finally appearing.

'You're so sure?'

'Come on,' she said. 'A bad divorce, she finally starts dating someone, he gets jealous and kills him.'

'But also shoots her?'

Hana was quiet for a moment.

'Angry, jealous man. It wouldn't be the first.'

Luke could see Hana's car parked illegally down the street, blocking an entire lane of traffic, the irritation of the drivers having to slow down and maneuver around it visible even from where they were standing.

'You love doing that, don't you?' Luke said, nodding towards the congestion.

'Best perk of the job.'

Luke checked the time and figured that Rowdy would be in the unit by now, so he fished his phone out of his pocket to ring her. Trevor Alpine's parents were due to arrive at his flat momentarily, having driven up from Dorset the night before, upset that they couldn't enter their son's home.

'Where did they stay?' Luke asked.

'We put them up at a hotel near London Bridge. But they are understandably angry,' Rowdy said.

'Okay, we'll head there now. Text the address please.'

Hana was surprised that the flat was still sealed off.

'Did the initial sweep find something?' she asked.

'Let's go find out.'

Luke told Hana to go ahead of him and move the car before it caused an accident while he made another quick call. As soon as she was out of earshot, he scrolled through his contacts and found the name of his therapist and pressed the call button.

The call went through to voicemail and Luke hesitated before hanging up. He didn't want to appear desperate or make a big deal about meeting with Nicky. It was going to be tricky enough to have the conversation in the first place. He sent her a brief text instead, explaining that he had returned to London early and was free to meet at his usual time on Monday morning if it was still available.

As he watched Hana get into the car and turn on the ignition, he wondered why he had not wanted her to hear him make this call. It was her text this morning that made him realize he did need to tell Nicky what was going on. Perhaps it was just too private, too difficult, too important. He pushed the thought out of his head and walked towards the car.

Luke's phone pinged with a text notification and he saw that Rowdy had sent the address. He could see Hana through the car window also looking at her phone, probably typing the location into the GPS directions.

'All okay?' Hana asked as Luke sat down in the passenger seat next to her.

'Yes, fine.'

Knowing not to push it, Hana pulled out of her convenient

parking spot and headed down Gower Street towards the Embankment. Traffic was still light, being a weekend morning, it made their drive south of the river much quicker than usual. Turning onto the street Rowdy had supplied, they didn't need the actual address. Two patrol cars both had their lights on, flashing like a strobe light in a disco, illuminating the entire street.

'Jesus,' Luke said.

Pulling up and parking illegally once again, Hana jumped out of the car and jogged over to what looked like an argument.

An older couple who Hana assumed were Trevor Alpine's parents were looking exasperated and shuffling between the building and a man who was shouting at four police officers. She flashed her identification at the officers and stepped directly between them and the man.

Luke watched this all unfold, still sitting in the car. He had learned that there was no point in stepping in here — Hana always beat him to it. He slowly unfastened his seat belt and opened the car door. The first words he heard being shouted were an obscenity in a woman's voice. Surprised, he realized that it was the mother, not Hana.

'Good morning everyone,' Luke said. 'Officers, please step this way.'

Reluctantly, three of the four officers, moved towards Luke, the final one stepping over to the parents and quietly saying something to them both with Hana in tow.

'I'm DCI Wiley, senior investigating officer on this case. I assume this is Mr and Mrs Alpine?'

A lanky officer cleared his throat.

'Yes, Sir.'

'And what the hell is going on?' Luke asked.

'I'm sorry, Sir. We were instructed to bring Mr and Mrs Alpine from their hotel to their son's flat and wait for you. I was told that Forensics is also attending today, but they haven't arrived yet.'

'And who is the shouting man?' Hana piped up.

'I didn't get the exact name. He said he is a colleague of the deceased and is kicking up a fuss about going into the flat — making threats with a lot of legal language, Sir.'

'What about you?' Luke asked the other officers.

'We heard the call for a disturbance and were only a couple of streets over. We came straight here.'

Luke took a deep breath and tried not to lose his temper. He could see from the look on Hana's face, standing with the parents, that she was also having a sense of humour failure about the situation.

'Officers, I'm not going to lecture any of you about the sensitivity needed here right now. These two people have lost their son less than forty eight hours ago. A son who was murdered. They are going to be upset. The colleague is going to be upset. And at this point, I am beginning to get upset because I cannot fathom why all of you couldn't contain a delicate situation without calling for assistance, naming a disturbance on a quiet Saturday morning, and leaving your patrol car lights on like we're in a war zone. For christ's sake, go and shut them off.'

The officers scattered without needing to be asked twice and Luke walked over to join Hana. He did not extend his hand as the gesture seemed barely adequate when confronting the grief that was etched into the faces of Mr. and Mrs. Alpine.

'Good morning. I am Detective Chief Inspector Luke Wiley. I am so sorry for your loss.'

'Thank you,' Mr. Alpine said quietly.

'And I'm sorry about the kerfuffle here. I'm afraid there is still a protocol in place for your son's flat and I've been instructed by the Forensic Team who will be here shortly that we may enter and speak inside, but not touch or move anything yet. I hope you understand.'

The man who had been shouting when Luke and Hana arrived strode over from the front door of the building where he had continued to be in discussion with the fourth officer.

'Good morning,' he said.

Hana and Luke both took a good look at him before replying.

He was handsome — not a typically helpful description in their line of work but it was the immediate word that came to mind. The man was tall, a chiselled face, slight cleft in his chin, and still a thick head of black hair for someone who looked to be in his mid-forties.

'I apologize for causing a scene. It was not my intention. Emotions are running high as you can imagine.'

'And you are?' Hana asked.

'My name is Morgan Lewis. I work with Trevor.'

'We called Morgan,' Mrs. Alpine said. 'We called him this morning hoping he had some sort of news or might have known what happened.'

Luke could see the Forensics van turning the corner onto the street, which was suddenly beginning to draw a small crowd of busybodies.

'Let's step inside,' Luke said, moving towards the building. 'Shall we?'

The five of them walked towards the entrance when the remaining officer who had stayed stationed at the front door stepped forward.

'Detectives?' he said.

Sensing that the officer was wanting to say something that he didn't want overheard, Luke and Hana excused themselves for a moment and stepped aside.

'What is it?' Luke said.

'I can't be sure,' the officer said, 'but when we arrived with

Mr. and Mrs. Alpine, I think I saw the colleague coming out of the building.'

'Did you question him?' Hana asked.

'Not exactly. I didn't want to seem insensitive and it was just out of the corner of my eye. So I asked him if he had a key to the building, as if we needed to get inside.'

'And what did he say?'

'He said he didn't, but I'm not sure I believe him.'

Luke nodded and thanked the officer. When he looked back towards the front door, Morgan Lewis was staring at him.

FOURTEEN

The building that housed Trevor Alpine's flat was a bit of an anachronism on the street. Although the area was full of new build construction, this particular street had maintained its Victorian buildings with their faded brick colour, detailed cornices and arched windows. Hana wondered how the planning permission for this building that contained six flats was granted. Although the height was the same as its neighbours, it stuck out like a sore thumb — all grey concrete and glass. She also wondered about the kind of person who would choose to live in this particular building.

A series of touchpoints that required a fob for entry — into the building, into the main door from the vestibule at the entrance, to press the lift button — led them upstairs to the third and top floor, each floor containing two flats that ran the length of the building on either side of the lift.

The police had already been through the flat once, their fob obtained from the building manager and their front door key to Trevor's flat created by the Met's handy locksmith. When the group got to the front door, Luke and Hana

purposely hung back to see if Morgan Lewis would offer his
own set of keys, but when he didn't, Luke unlocked the door.

Mrs. Alpine seemed slightly more stoic than her husband,
which was a bit of a surprise. Mr. Alpine choked back tears
that had come as soon as they stepped into his son's home.
The entrance hall was long and sparse with a polished concrete
floor and doors leading off it on both sides. Luke was aware of
not touching anything and instructed the others to do the
same. It was difficult to know where they should go to have
their conversation, so he asked Trevor's parents if there was a
room they would feel most comfortable in.

'The living room is the second door here on the left,' Mrs.
Alpine said. 'If I remember correctly. We've only been here a
couple of times.'

Luke led the way and the group assembled in the living
room, all standing awkwardly, not knowing whether to be
seated or not.

Morgan Lewis had joined them, not that he had been
invited and the detectives were torn between wanting to speak
privately to the grieving parents and curious enough about
Morgan's motives for being there that they wanted him to stay.
Luke decided to leave it up to the parents.

'Would you prefer that the four of us speak privately and
we can ask Mr. Lewis to wait with the Forensics Team?' Luke
said.

'No, it's fine. I think it better that we get as much information as we can at this point,' Mrs. Alpine said, squeezing her
husband's hand which hung limp at his side, his other hand
wiping away tears that he could not stop escaping.

Morgan smiled at Trevor's mother and moved to the side
so the rest of them could choose their seats. The living room
was large and contained three spacious sofas, the kind with
deep cushions so you could comfortably curl your legs up
underneath you and still have room to spare. The room looked

more like a hotel lobby than the living room of a flat and Hana wondered if Trevor Alpine hosted here a good deal, or was simply the kind of person who wanted to look impressive. It was difficult, and often unfair, to be judging a person in death by the surroundings they chose for themselves, but sometimes that was all they had to go on.

'Did Trevor recently move here and that's why you've only been here a couple of times?' Hana asked.

'No, Trevor has been here at least five years now, hasn't he?' Mrs. Alpine looked at her husband, who nodded. The use of the present tense struck everyone in the room.

'It's just,' she continued, trying to replace the shock she felt by what she had just said, 'usually Trevor came out to visit us in Dorset. He liked coming home and we saw him quite a bit there.' Her voice trailed off.

'I understand that this is an enormous shock to you, Mr. and Mrs. Alpine, and we are doing everything we can to understand the circumstances surrounding your son's death. We have some questions for you, and we are going to take a look around Trevor's flat ourselves, but before we begin, are there any specific questions that you may have that the officers who you've spoken to already have not covered?' Luke asked.

'Was it gang related? He was caught in crossfire? Or some sort of ritual and my son was shot?' Mr. Alpine said.

'We are still trying to determine the circumstances,' Luke replied.

'Surely CCTV will show who did this to my boy?'

'We have appeals out for any dash cam footage in the area, but there were no working cameras on that street that we can source.'

The parents were silent, taking this information in.

'When can I see him?' Mrs. Alpine said. 'I want to see Trevor.'

'Of course,' Hana said. 'We have arranged for support officers to be at your hotel after this interview and they will help you and take you where you need to be.'

'Thank you,' she whispered.

Luke shot a look at Hana to indicate that she was to take over here, sensing that they might get more information out of the mother than the father and she would respond better to a female detective. Luke turned to look at Morgan Lewis, who was sitting quietly, his hands in his lap and leaning forward, either out of respect or nervousness, he couldn't tell.

'We haven't been able to find out much about Trevor's private life,' Hana began. 'Had you met his girlfriend, Lisa Owen?'

'That is who he was with in the wine bar when he was killed?' Mrs. Alpine said.

'Yes, that's right. Have you met her? Know much about her?'

Mrs. Alpine looked a bit taken aback.

'Know much about her?' she said. 'I'd never even heard of her before this happened. Had you, Morgan?'

Everyone in the room turned to look at Morgan Lewis who took a moment to answer and cleared his throat.

'No, I hadn't met Lisa. But Trevor had mentioned her to me. I think it was very early days.' He paused, as if he was considering what to say next.

'Trevor dated quite a bit. All very casual. He chatted to me a bit about who he was seeing, but — how do I say this — he wasn't ready to settle down or anything, so the girls were all a bit....peripheral.'

Hana's face did not look impressed.

'Peripheral?' she said.

'Well, I mean that dating wasn't his priority. He was very focussed on his work. And of course he loved his family,' Morgan said, bowing his head slightly towards Trevor's parents.

Luke turned away from Morgan and directed his next question at the parents.

'What type of law did your son practice?'

'He was a litigator. Property mostly.'

'And you, Mr. Lewis?'

'I'm also in litigation.'

'How long have you known Trevor? Have you worked together for awhile?'

'About ten years, when Trevor joined the firm I work at. I had already been there for a couple of years. I can't tell you how much Trevor was liked at the company. He was an excellent solicitor and this is an enormous loss for us all.'

'Thank you, Morgan,' said Mr. Alpine, who had stopped crying, but was still holding his wife's hand.

'And you all know each other?' Luke asked, to no one in particular.

Mr. and Mrs. Alpine looked over at Morgan Lewis, who didn't return the gesture, staring instead at Luke and Hana as if he hadn't heard the question.

'No, actually,' said Mrs. Alpine. 'Well, we know of Morgan, of course. Trevor spoke of him all the time and for many years.'

'But you called him this morning?' Hana said.

'Yes. It just seemed like I should,' Trevor's mother replied. 'We feel so in the dark with everything and we wanted to speak to someone who knew our son well and maybe had a better sense of what was going on.'

Morgan smiled at the detectives, but said nothing in response.

The silence in the room was broken by the sound of a mobile phone ringing. It was Luke's and he pulled it out of his pocket.

'Excuse me for a moment,' he said when he saw the name

on the screen, standing up and stepping into the hallway before answering it.

'Good morning, Henry,' Luke said.

'Luke, the post has just arrived at the paper. I think there is another note.'

'Have you opened it?'

'No. But it's the same handwriting, same looking envelope. I called you right away.'

FIFTEEN

Rowdy picked up Luke's call before he even heard it ring on his end.

'Henry MacAskill just rang. He thinks he had received another note. I need you to..'

'Send Parker over there,' Rowdy interrupted. 'Got it.'

'Thanks.'

'Are you going to say it, or shall I?' Rowdy asked.

Luke had the feeling that this was coming. He let her have it.

'Go ahead,' he said.

'Thank goodness we have Officer Parker with us at the moment,' Rowdy said.

'Indeed. Thank you, Laura.'

Luke hung up and rejoined the others in the living room where Hana was quizzing everyone on Trevor's whereabouts for the few days prior to the shooting. Either they weren't being very forthcoming, or his whereabouts were simply not unusual. Work, home, they didn't really know.

With the Forensics Team now suited up and sweeping through the flat again, Luke and Hana instructed the Alpines and Morgan Lewis that they could stay put in the living room or head out for a coffee and they would be called when they could re-enter the flat at their leisure when the team was finished.

'Are you sure you want to let them back in here without supervision?' Hana asked.

'I'd like to have a good look around *without supervision*, wouldn't you?'

Hana nodded and once it was only the two detectives and the Forensics Team remaining, they began to look through every room.

'What are you looking for?' Hana said. 'You seem convinced that there is something here.'

'Well, that's the thing. There might be something here. If Morgan Lewis was in here before the Alpines arrived with the officer, he wouldn't have had much time. And the officer didn't see him with anything, so if he was looking for something specific, it's probably still in here.'

In addition to the large living room, the flat had a bedroom with ensuite, a guest bedroom that looked like it had been untouched for some time, a home office and another bathroom off of the kitchen.

'Bedroom first?' Hana said.

For a single man, the bedroom was relatively tidy. The bed was made, not all that neatly, but an effort had been made.

'Do you think he came home between work and meeting Lisa in the bar?' Luke said.

'Unlikely. The report said he was in a suit.'

Hana snapped a pair of latex gloves on and opened the wardrobe door. It looked like the average professional man's clothing rack — chinos, jeans, suits, shirts, jumpers on hangers, many pairs of expensive looking casual trainers. Next to the bed was a half empty glass of water, earplugs and a men's fitness magazine.

'Worth having Sharma check if he had a gym membership,' Hana said.

The bathroom was very clean, scattered with various grooming products and they noted again to check into a cleaner. There was no way that Trevor Alpine cleaned his flat himself to this level and with his work schedule. The only thing that revealed anything of Trevor's private life was an assortment of condoms in one of the bathroom drawers.

'He's having a lot of sex to have this much protection ready to go,' Luke said.

'Poor Lisa, I think she really thought she was the one.'

'If Trevor was not in touch with her for three weeks, he was probably seeing other women. Someone he shouldn't have been seeing? Your jealous husband theory?'

'What? That he was sleeping with someone who was married?'

'Could be.'

'God,' said Hana. 'Can you imagine being really into someone, thinking it's going really well, and not only is he not on the same page as you but he's actually shot and killed in front of you on your date?'

'How is this helpful, Hana?'

Hana shrugged.

'Just pointing it out,' she said.

The last room they entered was the home office. Trevor's laptop and iPad had already been removed and were back at the unit with Sharma and the other tech staff, so Luke and Hana shuffled through the papers and file folders on his desk. They were mostly indecipherable legal documents about cases that didn't mean anything to them. Copies would be made of them eventually.

'The wastepaper basket is empty,' Hana said. 'Did Forensics take out the contents already?'

Luke headed down the hall to speak to a member of the

team to find out. Hana tried the filing cabinet and to her surprise, it opened. She opened a couple of the folders inside and looked for a key, which is where she kept her key for the filing cabinet that she never bothered to lock. Somehow an unlocked filing cabinet in a flat as ordered and precise as Trevor Alpine's seemed unusual to her.

Hana opened the top drawer of the cabinet, which had no lock and there was very little in the drawer. Some sticky notes, a ruler, scissors, elastic bands, and a small pile of plastic cutlery and napkins, all emblazoned with different restaurant logos. Trevor obviously spent a lot of time ordering in and eating his meals while working at this desk.

Sliding her hand right to the back of the drawer, Hana touched a metal box and pulled it towards her. It was dark blue with a large clasp that snapped the box shut and released it open and you could carry it with a small handle. It looked older and was slightly battered, not fitting with the other new, sleek objects in the flat. The box was the size that could be used for petty cash, or could be something that held screws and nails and sat inside a toolbox. It looked like the kind of item that had been held onto for a long time, perhaps a couple of decades.

Hana popped the lid open and the smell hit her immediately. The scent was of a childhood pencil case, something that you would have carried with you in your school bag many years ago before the proliferation of laptops and other smart technology. It was a comforting, familiar, nostalgic smell.

Inside was a collection of pencils — some very old, their tips badly in need of sharpening. There were pens of all assortments. Ballpoints, ink nibs, felt pens, and a very expensive fountain pen that was not in its leather case. Some old stamps were stuck to the side of the box and looked like they had been put there on purpose, perhaps by a much younger Trevor Alpine.

Hana couldn't help but smile at the contents and felt suddenly enormously sad for the loss of this man who was shot on a date. The kind of man who would carry this keepsake box with him into his forties.

There were some coins in the bottom of the box — mostly pennies and some euro coins. Hana picked a couple of them up and took a closer look. One side of the euro coins she held in the palm of her hand was of a coat of arms she didn't recognize. There was a horse and a knight riding it and she tugged her mobile out of her pocket and took a photograph.

Dropping the coins back into the box, she noticed a bank note, also a euro note, tightly rolled up into a tube, as if it was trying to disguise itself as a writing instrument.

'Yes, they took the rubbish from this room and the kitchen on the first sweep,' Luke said, reappearing at the doorway.

Hana looked up at him.

'I'll bet you twenty quid that Dr. Chung's toxicology report is going to come back positive for cocaine. I have the feeling that Trevor Alpine was a complicated man.'

Sixteen

Bobby Sharma was the one member of the Incident Room team who had not left the building yet. He didn't really mind — he knew it was part of his job and it came with the territory. He had been so engrossed in the CCTV footage that he hadn't even noticed when one by one everyone else had left and at around two thirty in the morning, when he realized he was desperate to pee, he looked up and saw that he was suddenly alone.

He hoped that the rest of the team didn't think he was weird or unfriendly. He really tried to fit in with everyone and always went along to the pub after work with the colleagues he usually sat with one floor beneath this one, when he wasn't seconded to the Incident Room. He didn't even really drink, but always ordered a Strongbow in a pint glass so he looked just like everyone else.

Stretching and actually hearing the little bones in his shoulders click, he figured he needed to get up and get some blood pumping around his body again. He could have asked someone else to go over the camera footage with him and carry a bit of the load, but he was incredibly particular about his process. He knew that not only could he scan the screen for exactly what he was looking for more quickly than anyone else, but he had developed a specific algorithm once he had cycled through an hour of footage that sped up his frame views while not missing anything. He was quick and he was thorough, which is why he had been promoted so rapidly to be working with DCI Wiley on these kinds of cases in the first place. And more than all of this, even though his desire to fit in was an itch he always needed to scratch, the bottom line was that he preferred to work on these tricky parts of a case by himself. He got into the same kind of zone he used to inhabit when he was a teenager in his room, coding and programming and playing video games alone. It was a zone that was comfortable and he knew that it produced the best results.

He had also made a decision very quickly at around three o'clock in the morning and had abandoned the footage that had been sent in by the public from the first shooting on Thursday evening. It wasn't particularly good and there was simply too much footage to cover when they didn't even know what exactly they were looking for yet.

When he brought up the footage from Liverpool Street Station, he decided to focus on the one thing they did have — the victim. Four different cameras caught the execution of Alexander Mathison. It didn't matter how many times Sharma watched the footage. It was incredibly shocking.

If he had to admit something, it would be that the death itself wasn't all that shocking. A terrible thing to admit. Who hadn't become desensitized to this kind of violence? To watch a body fall to the ground from a single bullet that struck it was something that was now part of our psyche somehow, from films and television and the news and war conflicts and online games. This numbing to the death of a human being shouldn't happen, but it did.

What was shocking though was the venue and the familiarity of it. Sharma found himself winding the footage back to two minutes before the shooting, drawn into the normality of the scene. Weekday rush hour at a major transportation hub, streams of people exiting platforms in one direction and crowds of commuters moving in the opposite direction towards the trains. Friday night revellers entering the station and dispersing out of the two main exits. Luggage being wheeled behind people, heads looking up at the departure screens, heads bowed down towards mobile phones. It was all completely normal. It was an everyday scene repeated again and again at train stations all over the city, all over the country.

Sharma had slowed the footage down when he scrolled back, frame by frame, to watch Alexander Mathison enter the station. He had entered the concourse from the Bishopsgate entrance at the east of the station, descending the escalators by walking down the left hand side past the row of stationary passengers on the right. But he wasn't in a rush. Alexander stopped about twenty meters into the station and checked the departure board, then pulled his phone out of his inside coat pocket and looked at the screen. He didn't do anything else with the phone, only put it back from where he had removed it.

Sharma watched Alexander Mathison walk over to the sandwich kiosk and stand in line, moving his head and shoulders from side to side to see what was on offer behind the glass and that was being blocked by other customers in front of him. When it was his turn to pay, he didn't point to anything but spoke to the server and was handed a long paper tube that must have held a baguette. He did not buy anything to drink.

Alexander did not eat the baguette nor did he unzip his carryall and pop it inside to eat later on the train. Sharma pulled up the initial incident report that contained a detailed list of the bag's contents and photographs of the dead man on the concourse floor, as well as photos of the area around him.

There was no baguette. In the chaos that overtook the station when everyone realized someone had been shot, the sandwich which would have dropped out of his hands must have been kicked aside and probably shunted towards another part of the concourse. Why are you focusing on this silly detail, Sharma thought. Look at what matters first. Find the detail to fill in the blanks later.

When Alexander Mathison walked back towards the centre of the hall, he would have been facing the shooter who was standing directly at his twelve o'clock, just thirty five feet above him on the upper level. Did they make eye contact?

It didn't look like it.

Every single time Sharma watched this part of the play-back, he felt his body tense. It was as if he wanted to shout at the screen to not stand there, to move away and out of the shooter's line of sight.

It took only one second.

Alexander Mathison drops to the ground.

'Morning, Sharma.'

Sharma bolted out of his seat, an involuntary noise that could best be described as part whimper, part shriek came out of his mouth.

Luke found himself also jumping back at this reaction.

'Jesus, Sharma, are you alright?'

Sharma clutched the top of the chair he had just leapt out of, trying to compose himself.

'Sorry, Sir. I wasn't expecting you,' he said, a bit out of breath.

'Clearly,' said Hana from the doorway, watching the scene with amusement, before biting into a bagel that looked loaded with cream cheese.

'Where did you get that?' Luke said, turning around.

Hana's mouth was full and judging from the size of the

bite she just took, would take a few good seconds before she would be able to answer.

'Lombardi picked up breakfast,' Sharma said. 'I think she's just bringing it in now.'

Luke narrowed his eyes at Hana, although he shouldn't have been surprised that she got there first. Of course she did.

'I hear that you have something good to show us, Sharma,' Luke said.

'I do. A long night but a nice reward.'

'Well done.' Luke nodded at him. 'We need a break here.'

Lombardi appeared at the door, carrying a large cardboard box, the piece of tape on its seal already picked open so the lid was flapping up. Rowdy was close behind her.

'Should we wish to get a move on here, that would probably be wise. O'Donnell is in a meeting in his office but I can see that it's wrapping up and he's going to be straight over here,' she said.

Sharma moved back to his laptop and entered a few keystrokes that instructed his laptop screen to mirror onto the large screen next to the board at the front of the room where they had been assembling information.

'Okay,' he said. 'Here's Alexander Mathison at Liverpool Street last night. We catch him entering from the east, going about his business and then he was shot at 6:42pm.'

Everyone was silent as they took in the image on the screen in front of them. A man being executed in the middle of the station.

'Shit,' Lombardi said, surprising everyone in the room. But they knew what she meant. It was a shocking sight to witness.

'He knew what he was doing,' Hana said. 'That's a clean shot.'

'Continue please, Sharma,' Luke urged.

'I've got him all the way back to where he came from. Look at this,' Sharma said.

Frame by frame, Sharma did have him. The team watched the playback to see Alexander Mathison walk down Cheapside, most likely having emerged from his office, and turning left onto Bishopsgate before approaching the train station. He looked like every other commuter, completely unremarkable and completely unaware that his death was imminent.

But when he got to Liverpool Street station he did not enter it. The team watched Alexander turn in the opposite direction and walk towards Spitalfield Market.

'Good,' murmured Hana.

Luke knew what she meant. They might finally have something to work with and that market was full of CCTV cameras. Sure enough, they watched him weave through the after work crowds that were beginning to swell at that time on a Friday evening and duck into the market. Sharma clicked his mouse a couple of times and the image on the screen jumped forward in time a few seconds to catch up with Alexander, now heading into a tapas restaurant on the outer edge of the market.

'It's called Buenos Tiempos,' Sharma said. 'He's in there for just over and hour and then comes out and straight to the station. And...we've seen that footage.'

'Excellent work Sharma,' Luke said.

'Thank you, Sir. Except that's not all.'

Luke looked expectantly at him, waiting for Sharma to continue.

'I've got the shooter on camera, too.'

SEVENTEEN

As soon as Sharma said it, Lombardi dropped the pen she had been unconsciously gripping in her hand and the thwack it made on the hard floor of the Incident Room, made everyone jump. The room had been silent, intensely focused on the slightly grainy footage — also in silence — of Alexander Mathison in the moments before his death. It was clear that the team was on edge.

'Sorry,' she said.

'You have him?' Luke asked. 'I thought he was smart enough to be standing in a blind spot and there was no CCTV of the bastard.'

'He was that smart,' Sharma replied. 'But then he had to get out of the station.'

'You didn't want to start with this?' Hana asked, a little incredulously.

Luke couldn't help but smile.

'DS Sawatsky, what do I always say?'

Hana glared at him and did not reply. The others in the room may have thought she was being prickly because Luke had called her by her formal name, but she knew he did this to tease her. This was the reason for the hard stare.

Never begin with the best part. Luke was insufferable with his favourite motto. The one that always ended up getting the most important details out of someone in an interrogation. The one that he lived by. The one that Hana knew, when applied to his personal life made him unbearably sad. His best part was with Sadie, was at the beginning of his life, and now it was over.

Sharma, not understanding the unspoken exchange between the two detectives, cleared his throat. Luke turned his attention back to the screen.

'Go ahead, Sharma.'

'Right,' Sharma said. 'We pick him up easily, actually. Watch this.'

They watched the screen, all of them waiting to see something sinister, someone who looked guilty. But this is not what they saw.

It was obvious from the footage, even without any sound, that the gunshot that rang out in the middle of a busy train station got a little bit of notice, but not much. There didn't seem to be any immediate panic, any rush towards the exits. That came about two minutes later. Hana was staring at the running time stamp in the corner of the screen, in amazement that it took this long for anyone to understand what had happened.

'Not yet,' murmured Luke, who was unconsciously moving closer to the screen. His muttering announcing aloud what they were all thinking.

The shooter hadn't shown himself yet.

He must have been watching.

The camera did not show it, because he had cleverly stood exactly where he could not be seen. But he was watching. The shooter would have been standing in the same position as where he took his shot, looking down as his victim below, bleeding out on the cold, concrete floor. Did he slip his gun back into his coat pocket, unnoticed? Did he say anything as he stood there? Did he smile?

They were never to know.

Sharma left this footage running for a moment. It would have been an excellent lesson in crowd reaction, perhaps taught on a course to explain the human response to an unanticipated traumatic event. Everything looked normal and then it was as if movement in the crowd slowed down a beat. Perhaps someone had screamed. Someone called for help. Someone realized that Alexander Mathison had been shot and shouted that someone had a gun. Whatever it was, they all watched the understanding of the past few seconds trickle through the station. And then people started to run.

'If this is our guy,' said Sharma, 'and I'm going by the witness description. He's the only guy in a hoodie on the upper level that I see within 45 seconds of the shooting, then here he is.'

Luke was now right up at the screen, willing this bastard to show his face.

But they weren't that lucky.

The shooter was of average height and it was slightly difficult to get an accurate sense of his build due to the dark coat he was wearing over his hoodie, the hood pulled up over his head. What they were seeing was a cold blooded killer. An executioner calmly walking away from the scene, matching the quicker pace of the people around him.

But he wouldn't have stood out at that moment as anyone extraordinary.

Hana said what everyone was thinking.

'He looks like he fits in. I mean, in that part of town. He obviously didn't come from an office, like Alexander Mathison. But the clothes — they look cool. Like he works in fashion or advertising or something. What is that coat? Tweed? It looks expensive. And the hood up could be just that it's December and it's cold.'

'What kind of shoes?' Lombardi asked.

Hana squinted at the screen. They looked like leather boots.

'Military, do you think?' said Lombardi.

Hana shook her head.

'Doubt it. No laces that I can see in this angle. Let's keep going please, Sharma.'

Sharma clicked his mouse again and they watched the shooter exit the station with the rest of the crowd and walk past the taxi rank, past the fast food outlets and towards Finsbury Pavement. Sharma kept clicking his mouse and they waited for the shooter to do something — pull out his gun again, remove his hood so they could get a better look at him, jump into a getaway car. What they weren't expecting is for the killer to pop into the pub.

'Are you serious?' Luke said.

'If this is our guy,' Sharma replied, 'he went for a goddamn pint.'

The entire team looked back towards the screen and the Dog and Duck pub. It would have been a bit of a grungy train station pub, not exactly the Draper's Arms where Luke and Henry had met the night before.

'And when does he come out? Can you forward to that footage please?'

'Well that's the thing,' Sharma said. 'He doesn't come out.'

'What? Ever?' Hana said.

Sharma nodded and leaned back in his chair, his palms upturned in frustration.

The person who sighed the loudest at that point was Laura Rowdy. She didn't like this situation at all. Too many leads which meant too many dead ends and she had the feeling that they didn't have a lot of time.

'DCI Wiley,' she said.

Luke knew that she addressed him like this not to match how he had just teased Hana, but to get him to snap to attention. To do what needed to be done and something that he hated doing. He was going to have to delegate.

Luke's internal, inaudible sigh would have dwarfed the one just made by Rowdy. He hated delegating, and he knew this was a weakness in his leadership style. He trusted his colleagues implicitly and relied on them completely. He just hated the feeling of not being the one to uncover the information.

Hana used to tease him about this — this fear of missing out. It was a bit inexplicable to her and couldn't help but make her laugh. Luke was someone who loved spending time on his own away from other people. She just knew that he was a bit of a control freak. And right now in the Incident Room, she could see it playing out across his face.

'Okay,' Luke said. 'First of all, has Parker come back from the paper yet with whatever was delivered to Henry?'

'He should be back any second,' Rowdy said. 'But rather more pressing is Amelia Mathison. She has returned to London with support officers from Suffolk and has gone home. She is expecting you this morning.'

'I can go,' Hana offered.

'We'll both go,' said Luke.

'So, that leaves the two of you,' Luke said, looking at Lombardi and Sharma.

Lombardi finally put the cap back on her pen and nodded, ready to head out. But Sharma usually stayed put in the station, piecing together everything that the team brought in for analysis. He wasn't a field officer.

'You are now,' Luke said, when Sharma pointed this out.

'The tapas restaurant and the Dog and Duck are only a five minute walk from each other. I'll let you decide the order. Report back here as soon as you can.'

'Yes, Sir,' said Sharma.

Luke drained the last of his coffee and looked back at the screen, the last image of the back of the killer frozen there.

'My Spanish isn't great,' Luke said. 'What does Buenos Tiempos mean?'

'It means Good Times,' said Lombardi.

Luke winced slightly.

'Not exactly what Alexander Mathison had last night.'

EIGHTEEN

B y eleven o'clock, the sun had been out for over three hours and had warmed up what would otherwise have been a very chilly December day. He was glad that the weather had turned out like this on a Saturday when he wasn't stuck in the office.

His springer spaniel was even happier. The dog always knew when it was a weekend and his walk would be coming later in the day because he was still home and had simply opened the back door to the tiny patio garden with it's one strip of grass to let the dog have his morning pee there.

'Come on, Douglas, shall we head off?' he said to his canine companion.

Usually, he would walk south on Queen's Gate, past the museums and towards the busier shopping streets of Chelsea. They had a routine — pick up whatever weekend paper looked the most interesting from the copy on the front page, usually the Times, at the store on the corner of his road and stop for a coffee and a danish at the little Scandinavian coffee shop on Sloane Street. He liked to sit at one of the metal tables outside on the pavement and watch the world go by, with Douglas at his feet.

There used to be a barista there who loved Douglas and gave him a small treat from a glass bowl under the counter, but she had left now to return home. He found it strange that he missed this tiny interaction so much.

But this routine could wait today. He had slept well and felt invigorated and this sunny day deserved something more than just the usual. So he slipped the clasp of the lead onto the opposite one on the dog's collar and headed out the door, turning north towards the park.

He did love living so close to Hyde Park and it was one of the reasons he chose this particular flat, the compromise being that it was on the lower ground floor. He walked in Hyde Park most days with Douglas, around the hours of his office job and he liked to alternate the routes they used. Sometimes they headed directly to the Serpentine and did that circular walk, the dog enjoying the ducks and geese that he liked to bother. Douglas was a friendly dog, never barking at the water fowl but probably wanting to join them. He found his dog's good nature to be fortunate, because all of the training in the world wouldn't fix a snappy, calculating canine. Humans were like this too, of course. Politeness never truly masked a terrible personality.

As they crossed Kensington Gore, the man looked towards the Royal Albert Hall, a building he had not been in since he was a child. He couldn't remember what concert he attended with his mother and his sister, but it was in the early spring — probably during the Easter break — and he had loved it. He does remember the grandeur of the building inside, it's circular design enveloping them and the delight of all of the boxes dotted around the upper balcony, staring down at the spectators below. He had been sitting in the stalls and remembers feeling like he was also on display, in the way that is exciting only to a child.

It had been a day trip into London for this event and he wishes that he could remember more about it and why they had come in to see the concert. When he moved to London for work many years later, he had planned to go back to the Royal Albert Hall and see something — a Christmas concert, or something at the Proms in the summer. But life takes over and he had never gotten around to it.

When he married, he was sure that he would take his own child to see something and he remembers telling his wife this. It was one of their many plans, something they could see in front of them in the not too distant future. This was maybe the best time of his life, the man thought as he continued on into the park, cutting left towards Kensington Palace. This time of possibility and of security.

He had met his wife not too far from here, in fact, although he didn't live in this part of London then. He had met her in the most usual and predictable way — at the pub. He hadn't even wanted to go out that afternoon but had been persuaded by a couple of friends to meet them for lunch in a pub in Edwardes Square. He had nothing better to do, so he joined them and the extra couple of pints at the bar afterwards had led to an introduction to a friend of a friend of someone he had bumped into. Looking back now it all seemed so implausible, but it had felt like magic at the time.

He pushed the thought out of his head because what was the point. The marriage had not led to children and had ended with a whimper a few years later. He probably wasn't the marrying type, she had said as they divided up their belongings in the split. Who was he to argue with that? She was probably right.

Life is full of small disappointments and he did his best not to let them add up into something greater than himself. His life was steady and interesting enough and he did just fine. The life that would have had more magic — concerts with his children at the Royal Albert Hall — did not materialize and that was fine, too.

Douglas pulled on the lead and whined and the man realized that his pace had slowed, irritating the dog.

'Sorry, Douglas,' he said.

Walking a bit more briskly now, the man admired the winter roses still in bloom in the Palace Gardens, just visible from the path. Whatever one thought of the royal family, he had to admit that their parks were glorious and the gardens a treat to walk around. It was uplifting to see something so beautiful still alive and flowering as the cold winter began to close in on them.

'Shall we head to the trees, Douglas?'

The dog looked up at him and wagged his tail.

'Come on, boy.'

The man smiled at the dog as they turned east and headed towards the small thicket of trees in the north west corner of the park. Douglas loved to run around there and sometimes the man would let him off the lead here if there was no one else around to complain. The dog was well behaved and the man never worried that he would run off and not return.

When they reached the trees there was only one other person there, another dog walker who had already let his dog off the lead and the man decided it would be best to keep Douglas on his.

'Good morning,' he said.

'Oh good morning.'

The man recognized the other dog walker — he had seen him before, perhaps a couple of weeks earlier.

'I'm sorry, I'll call him back,' the dog walker said, and whistled for his own dog, who obediently returned and was put back on his lead.

'Beautiful day,' the dog walker said.

'Yes.'

The two men chatted for a minute about nothing in particular. No one overheard them. And no one saw the long barrelled revolver that he pulled out of his coat, pressed to the back of the dog walker's head as he bent down to adjust the dog's collar, and pulled the trigger.

The lead was still wrapped around the dog walker's hand and the other man gently untied it. The dead man's dog sat very still.

Picking up both leads, he walked away from the trees and back towards the Serpentine, not looking back.

NINETEEN

Officer Parker was out of breath as he arrived back at the station. He was so desperate to get upstairs with the note, sealed in an evidence bag, that he didn't wait for the lift. He bounded up all seven flights of stairs, not encountering a single other person because no one would be daft enough to climb up or down the stairs in Scotland Yard.

When he had arrived at the paper, he wasn't sure what to expect as he had never been in a newsroom before. He had seen old American films that his dad had liked about newsrooms in the sixties and seventies, all cigarette smoke and piles of paper and the clacking sound of typewriter keyboards.

The newsroom at the paper was nothing like this. There wasn't a typewriter in sight and he felt stupid that he was surprised by this. He couldn't even get into the reception area of the building without showing identification in the lobby and passing through security metal detectors like he was going to board an airplane. The intern who had come downstairs to collect him at least looked excited to be dealing with a police officer.

'Is this about the shooting at the station last night?' he had asked Parker as they were in the lift. The building was so tall and the lift was moving so quickly that Parker could feel his ears popping. He swallowed hard and hoped that the intern didn't notice.

'I'm not at liberty to say, I'm afraid.'

The intern nodded solemnly and Parker hoped that he had gotten away with using this kind of language. He couldn't believe that the words had just burst out of his mouth as if he said them all the time, and wasn't slightly pretending that he was in a film himself.

Parker wondered exactly how many reception desks there were in this building, even more than at Scotland Yard, which was hard to believe. He was made to wait again until a tall, slightly balding man with round tortoiseshell glasses came out to greet him. Unlike the intern who was wearing a smart suit and polished black leather shoes, this man was in jeans, a navy jumper and brown suede desert boots. Parker noticed that his laces were untied as if the man had just slipped them on to trundle out to reception to fetch him.

'Good morning,' the man said.

'Hi,' said Parker, wondering if they even knew why he was here.

'Um,' Parker continued, 'Laura Rowdy sent me?'

The man smiled a warm, friendly smile.

'Of course she did. Come through, please.'

Parker followed the man into an enormous room that looked like it took up the entire floor of the building. The intern excused himself and disappeared down a rabbit warren of desks to the left and in front of them were not the cubicles that Parker had been expecting, but long tables in a series of rows that were sort of aligned, but seemed to fan out from a central point in the room. Each table housed at least half a dozen computer stations, most of them occupied by journalists typing away. Some had headphones on, some were quietly talking on the phone. Parker was shocked at how quiet a room could be with this many people in it. The frenetic energy from the movies did not exist in here.

'I'm just back here,' the man said before turning around to take a look at Parker. 'I'm Henry MacAskill, by the way. And you are?'

'Parker, Sir.'

'Do you have a first name, Parker?'

'Tom, Sir.'

Henry stopped and turned to look at Parker, a little smile dancing on his lips. He couldn't be more than twenty six or twenty seven years old, a strapping young man with the kind of hair that made him jealous. It was plentiful and a great shade of brown and was so thick, in fact, that it sort of bounced when Parker walked, even with its short cut. Henry was curious to understand why Rowdy trusted him enough to send him over to obtain such a crucial piece of evidence.

Continuing through the newsroom, he could see Parker taking everything in and they arrived at Henry's little office at the back of the floor. Not unlike the offices on the Serious Crimes Unit, it was enclosed by glass but unlike at Scotland Yard, this office did not have blinds you could shut. It was completely transparent and Henry could be seen by the rest of the newsroom at all times.

Henry didn't ask Parker to be seated and he stood there awkwardly, suddenly feeling nervous that he was going to screw up this simple task of retrieving the evidence and returning it as quickly as possible to the station.

'You're in uniform,' Henry said. 'Are you a detective in training?'

Parker wasn't sure how to answer this. He wasn't entirely sure what he was doing back in the Incident Room with the rest of the Serious Crime Unit team, but he had been thrilled to get the call from Rowdy that morning. His sergeant wasn't exactly pleased, both irritated that he had another roster to fill and jealous that Parker was being singled out by a rank far, far above him.

'To be honest, I'm not sure,' Parker said, with a smile that he hoped was reassuring.

'And how did you get seconded by DCI Wiley?'

'I first met DCI Wiley on the Grace Feist case,' he said.

'I see,' Henry replied, moving around his desk and taking a seat. 'How is that?'

'I was the responding officer when the body was found in the canal and it sort of went from there.'

'You continued working with DCI Wiley on the case after that?'

'Yes, Sir.'

'Do you know why?'

'Why what, Sir?'

Henry pursed his lips and smiled again at the young man.

'Why,' Henry said, 'you continued to work on the Grace Feist case if you are not actually a detective.'

Parker couldn't help but bristle at this last comment. He had been asked to work with the team on the Grace Feist case just as he had been asked to dash over to the paper to retrieve an important piece of evidence and try to determine anything else he could about where it had come from. Why this journalist was questioning him like this was beyond him. It was pissing him off.

'I saved DS Sawatsky's life, Sir. So I suppose they think I'm useful.'

At this, Henry's head snapped up, which had been momentarily distracted by an email he had caught out of the corner of his eye, sitting unopened in his inbox on the computer monitor in front of him.

'You were the officer who broke into the house where she was being held?'

'After I figured out the connection with Caitlin Black.'

Henry raised his eyebrows and stood up again.

'Well then I'd say you are an integral part of their team, wouldn't you?'

'I'm not sure I would say one way or another, Sir,' replied Parker. 'But I am here to retrieve a note you have received. Do you have it?'

Henry pointed to a large sack that was sitting on the floor next to his desk. It was a Royal Mail branded, dirty white sack that looked like it had been tossed around in the back of lorries, dragged along filthy floors and abused in a myriad of ways.

'This is what the post for this floor arrived in. My post is taken out first by the intern — you met him coming in. Once I saw the envelope that was the same as the one I received yesterday which Luke — sorry DCI Wiley — already has, I put it down here and rang Wiley immediately. I haven't opened it.'

Parker looked down at the desk and at the unassuming white envelope with Henry's name and the postal address of the newspaper in handwriting across the front.

'I didn't allow the rest of the post to be distributed, in case you needed to go through it,' Henry said, nodding towards the dirty sack.

Parker was grateful for the latex gloves that Rowdy had reminded him to take along and pulled them out of his pocket. As he struggled to shove his fingers into them, he asked where the mailroom was.

'It's in the basement. I can take you down there, if you'd like.'

The note safely sealed in the evidence bag, Parker opened the sack and to his relief saw that it was only a quarter full. He went through the post and Henry stood looking over his shoulder. As far as they could tell, there was nothing out of the ordinary. He folded the empty sack to take with him, just in case, and thanked Henry for his help.

As Parker went to leave, ready to be escorted by the intern to the mailroom before heading back to Scotland Yard, Henry stopped him and opened his mouth to say something, hesitating just slightly.

'Parker, you seem like a good kid.'

'Thank you, Sir?'

Henry laughed softly at the inflection in Parker's voice, unsure if what he said was to be taken as a compliment or not.

'It's important that you keep an eye on DCI Wiley and DS Sawatsky. They may be in for quite a ride here.'

'Yes, Sir,' said Parker, not entirely understanding the meaning behind Henry's words.

———

The mailroom in the bowels of the building didn't provide much more information. Parker took note of how the post was delivered to the building but it was mostly sorted into the sacks by the postal service before arriving at the paper. It was possible that the barcode on the empty sack might be able to give a bit more detail if Sharma could work his magic, but Parker wanted to get back to the station as quickly as possible.

He had been disappointed that the letter was not yet opened as he had hoped to have a head start on figuring out what the contents meant before the others saw it in the Incident Room. He felt silly for being so selfish, or for thinking that he alone was going to crack this case, but he was desperate to prove his worth in that room.

By the time he arrived back at Scotland Yard, he felt slightly frantic and when the lifts were both taking an absolute age to make their way down to the ground floor, he abandoned them and began to sprint up the stairs.

Catching his breath as he walked down the corridor on the seventh floor towards the back of the unit where the Incident Room was located took him longer than he would have liked. He was just in time to catch DCI Wiley and DS Sawatsky step out of the room, both of them craning their necks towards O'Donnell's office, hoping to slip by unnoticed.

'Jesus, Parker, are you alright?' Hana said when she noticed him striding towards them. 'Your face is the colour of a lobster that's just been pulled out of the pot.'

Luke turned to his partner.

'A lobster?'

Hana shrugged.

'First thing that came to mind.'

'How did it go, Parker?' Luke asked.

'I have it, Sir.'

Luke looked at Rowdy and Hana, really needing to get to Amelia Mathison, but needing to know what was in this note even more.

'Okay, let's open it in the Incident Room. Do you have a letter opener, Rowdy?'

She nodded and went to fetch it.

'Did Henry say anything else about the note?' Luke asked.

'About the note? No.'

Hana frowned.

'What did he say, Parker?'

Parker hesitated, suddenly feeling out of his depth with these two detectives. He was sure that he was going to be sent back to his patrol now. They were going to want him out of the way.

'It's nothing. He just said that I should look out for you because this was a difficult case.'

Luke and Hana didn't say anything and Parker didn't

know how to react. Instead, he focused his attention on the evidence bag he was still holding in his hands.

'Right,' said Luke. 'Let's take a look, shall we?'

Snapping on a pair of gloves, Luke took the letter opener that was handed to him by Rowdy, and unzipped the evidence bag. He pulled out the envelope and carefully inserted the tip of the penknife, tugging it slowly down the seal until the paper revealed an open seam.

'God I feel like you're opening my exam results,' Hana said.

No one said anything in response. They didn't need to because they all felt the same.

Luke pulled out the contents of the envelope and like the previous one Henry received, it was a single piece of paper, unfolded, clearly cut to size to fit the envelope. This one wasn't handwritten, but had been put through a printer. The type wasn't exactly centered on the page, skewing slightly to the bottom.

Choo, Choo
I shot you
Those who are naughty
Must be punished

Twenty

'Would you like to drive?' Sharma asked Lombardi, hoping desperately that she would say yes. He barely drove at all, even though he had passed his driving test over a decade earlier. He had grown up on the outskirts of London and thought it was a skill he should learn, but once the goal of getting the license was achieved, he found that he didn't enjoy it. And now he lived in a city with one of the best public transportation systems so never really needed to drive anywhere, even when he went home to visit his parents.

'Sure,' she said.

Lombardi had actually taken the Metropolitan Police driving course, even though an analyst would rarely have cause to use the skills she learned in it. It was a hell of a lot of fun and she felt thrilled to be handed a set of car keys and let loose into the city. She hoped that Sharma hadn't noticed.

As they drove towards Spitalfields Market, Sharma and Lombardi made a bit of small talk. Although they worked with each other most days, and every day when called into the Incident Room, they both realized that they didn't actually know the other very well. Hours of the day spent in the same place didn't exactly reveal a lot about a person, as much as one may think.

'I wasn't expecting this to be part of my day,' Sharma said. 'I thought I'd be chained to video footage.'

'I suppose that DCI Wiley wants to keep everything in close quarters. Easier to keep tabs on everything if its the same team, as opposed to bringing in a ton of other new people to work on it.'

'Yes,' said Sharma.

The unspoken words between them were how pleased they were that this was the case. That Sharma and Lombardi were the chosen ones, the people DCI Wiley trusted.

'What do you think of Wiley and DS Sawatsky?' Lombardi suddenly asked.

'What do you mean?'

'I don't know,' Lombardi said. 'They seem really close. I've never worked with anyone else at the Met who seem to be such good friends.'

'I guess I've never really thought about it,' Sharma said.

'Right.'

Lombardi turned up towards Liverpool Street Station when they reached the north side of London Bridge. Mid-morning traffic was busy and they inched forward as every traffic light they approached seemed to turn red the moment they got there. She thought about turning on the flashing lights and having the cars around them move out of the way, but then thought that may be a step too far in this situation. Was this considered an emergency? Probably, but she was too nervous to try it.

'Had you worked with Wiley and Sawatsky before the Grace Feist case?' Sharma asked.

'No. You?'

'No.'

The two colleagues were slightly shy with each other, looking for common ground in this space that was unfamiliar to them. Lombardi liked Sharma a great deal — he was excellent at his job, and kind, and very occasionally quite funny. She stole a quick glance at him, hoping that he thought she was checking the mirror on his side. He looked up from his phone at her just when she did this and smiled.

'What do you think of O'Donnell?' Sharma said. He was very clear about what he thought — the guy was an asshole, but largely stayed out of his way. If he continued to progress up the hierarchy ladder at the Met, Sharma wondered if this would still be the case. But never wanting to assume that his opinions were the same as someone else's, he felt it safer to ask the question.

'Oh, he's a right prick,' Lombardi said.

Sharma couldn't help but laugh.

'No kidding.'

Lombardi wondered what to do here — should she say something? She felt anxious about her exchange with O'Donnell that morning and beyond that, had no idea what it meant. She took another quick look at Sharma. Could she trust him?

'Actually,' she said, 'something happened with O'Donnell this morning. It might have been nothing, but it was strange.'

Sharma put his phone back in his pocket, shifting in his seat to do so.

'What happened?'

Lombardi described the conversation — or the one-sided conversation, and everything that O'Donnell had said to her and what he had asked her to do.

'He wants you to spy on Wiley and Sawatsky? What the hell for?'

'I don't know,' Lombardi said, pulling up in front of the Dog and Duck and putting the car into park.

'And, don't take this the wrong way,' Sharma said, 'but why is O'Donnell asking *you*?'

At this question, Lombardi's stomach flipped. She hadn't really thought this through. Why was she being targeted? And what was this going to mean for her job if she didn't come through for him?

Sharma sensed that her silence masked something she didn't want to say or was too nervous to try, so he didn't push it any further and pointed towards the market.

'The Dog and Duck is on that corner. Let's see what we can find.'

Grateful to not be talking about O'Donnell any further, Lombardi got out of the car and pressed the key fob to lock the doors behind them. It was, she had to admit, very freeing to be able to just leave the car where they parked it and not look for a ticket machine or worry about being fined. If only her entire life was like that.

The Dog and Duck was one of those pubs that had a perpetually sticky floor. Even the best industrial steam cleaner wasn't going to get a few decades worth of spilt pints, sweaty commuters and god knows what else off of that floor.

When he was at university, there were a group of guys that Sharma hung around with who liked to go to pubs like this one. Slightly rougher than their social class so it made them feel cool to go in and sink a few beers. But Sharma never felt very cool in the first place and the smell of the pub was unbearable to him after awhile.

This pub smelled exactly the same, he thought when they walked in the door.

'I'm surprised it's open already,' said Lombardi. 'It's only ten thirty in the morning.'

'I think the kind of clientele they get in here like to start early.'

There were a couple of old geezers in the corner, but the pub was otherwise empty.

Lombardi and Sharma walked towards the barman who was drying some wine glasses with a tea towel, when Lombardi suddenly stopped.

'What is it?' Sharma asked.

'Do we, like, show ID or something?'

Sharma grinned at her.

'Oh this is the part I've been waiting for,' he said, as he reached into the inside pocket of his jacket to pull out his identification, which Lombardi realized to her amusement that he had already removed from his wallet for this exact purpose.

'Metropolitan Police,' Sharma said as loudly as he could get away with, without looking foolish.

The barman barely looked up.

'Good morning,' said Sharma, a little quieter this time. 'I'm Detective Constable Sharma and this is DC Lombardi.'

Sharma threw a quick look at Lombardi — a slight apology as he knew that this was not her technical rank, but introducing her as Analyst didn't seem like it was going to get them very far in this situation. They needed to come back to the Incident Room with what Wiley and Sawatsky needed.

'What can I do for you?'

'We're here about the shooting last night in the station. We have reason to believe that the shooter came into this pub during the evening.'

That got the barman's attention and he set down the wine glass he was holding.

'You don't say.'

'Can we have a look at your CCTV please?' Sharma asked.

'We've only got the one camera mate,' the barman said, pointing directly behind them to an ancient looking camera in the corner of the ceiling, facing the bar.

'Do you have the footage here? On tape or...?'

'Sure, we have a tape. Come with me.'

The barman led them into a back storage room that was even filthier than the public area. Lombardi shivered as she looked around.

'It's all here. I take it you'll know how it works. Help yourself,' the barman said, and then left them to it.

Sharma hadn't seen a system this old in quite some time. He fiddled around with it — at least it was being recorded on a CD and not a cassette — and brought up the footage from the previous evening.

They spotted the shooter immediately.

TWENTY-ONE

The camera footage was decent enough and Lombardi and Sharma watched the continuation of what they already had from the station and the street cameras back at Scotland Yard.

The shooter still had the long tweed coat on over his hoodie, the hood up around head, obscuring any decent view of him. He walked straight past the bar and through the hallway towards the bathrooms.

Lombardi cursed audibly as they watched him do this, knowing there was no camera back there. They kept the footage rolling, waiting for the shooter to appear again after having relieved himself. After three minutes, he still hadn't reappeared.

'Maybe executing someone during rush hour really makes you have to go,' Lombardi said.

Sharma was only half paying attention to her, his eyes lasered in on the image in front of them.

They watched the tape for a full ten minutes. The shooter did not reappear.

'What the hell,' Sharma said. 'Let's go take a look.'

Their chairs scraped backwards on the wood floor, making Lombardi's teeth ache, and the pair walked into the hallway which had both a mens and ladies bathroom.

'Do you want to check yours and I'll do the same?' Sharma said.

Lombardi nodded and popped into the ladies. She would guess that it was infinitely cleaner than the one Sharma was checking out. There was no window and no other exit. Sharma confirmed the same when he came out of the mens.

The only other way out was another door that led from the hallway to the rubbish collection area, which in turn led to the street.

As they stood outside, the smell of the enormous metal rubbish bin nauseating them both, they felt utterly defeated. This is how the shooter got away.

Sharma thanked the barman as they left, the CD footage from the evening before safely in their possession to examine in better detail back in the Incident Room.

'Maybe we'll have more luck at the tapas restaurant,' Lombardi said, trying to sound as encouraging as possible.

Sharma and Lombardi could see that Buenos Tiempos was quite a large restaurant as they approached it, deceptively so.

'That's a good sign,' Sharma said, as Lombardi commented on its size. 'Means they very likely have some better CCTV than the pub.'

They approached the door where they could see staff setting up inside, but no patrons yet as it was still a little early for lunch. Sharma knocked on the door, startling the young man setting out cutlery and glasses on the tables. When the young man signalled to his watch as if to mime that they weren't open yet, Sharma took this as his cue to whip out his ID again.

'We are investigating the shooting at the station last night and we have reason to believe that the victim ate here earlier in the day.'

'Really? Oh my god,' the young man said.

'May we speak to you and any other staff who are present?' Lombardi said.

'Yes, of course.'

Three other members of staff were in the restaurant and two of them had also been working the evening before. Lombardi brought up the driver license photograph of Alexander Mathison on her phone and showed it to them.

'Yes,' said the young man. 'I served him last night I think. It was just after office hours, right? He was here with a woman.'

'Can you describe the woman?' Lombardi asked.

'I don't really remember much. She was pretty, maybe thirty? A little younger?'

Sharma had already spotted the CCTV cameras in the restaurant, helpfully in all corners, so the entire place would have been covered.

'Do you have the camera footage from these?' he asked, pointing upwards.

'Yes,' said his colleague. 'They are on the laptop in the back room — not all that sophisticated, but we will have it all. It doesn't erase for thirty days.'

'I'll come back and have a look now,' Sharma said, nodding at Lombardi to continue without him.

'I appreciate that you wouldn't have been paying particular attention to these two people last night, but did anything stick out for you about them?' Lombardi asked the other three staff members.

All of them shook their head.

'I don't think they were here very long,' said the young man.

'Will you still have those receipts handy?' Lombardi asked.

'Sure,' he said. 'They were sitting here at the window table, so that's station twelve. I'll get the receipts from twelve for you. Hold on a sec.'

In the backroom, which was really no more than a glorified cupboard holding a desk and a stool and a laptop hiding amongst stacks of paper that looked like supply orders, the woman who seemed to be in charge of everyone else logged into the computer.

'Is it cloud based?' Sharma asked.

'Yes, we pay a subscription service so I just need to go into their website and last night's footage will be there. We have three cameras in that front room.'

'And anywhere else?'

'Above the bar,' she replied. 'In case any of the staff have sticky fingers, but in general we never have any problems with that.'

'Were you working last night?' Sharma asked.

'No, sorry, I wasn't. It's so terrible what happened to that man. Do you know who shot him?'

Sharma wondered what answer DCI Wiley would give here, and he tried to channel his boss.

'We're getting all of our facts together and we will let the public know the exact circumstances just as soon as we can,' he said, hoping that he sounded convincing.

'Yes, of course,' the woman replied.

She clicked through into the surveillance website and Sharma thanked the gods that it was all there and the footage was surprisingly refined for such an inexpensive system.

'Do you know what time you're looking for?'

'Would you mind if I had a go?' Sharma said.

'Be my guest,' the woman replied, stepping back to let Sharma into the tiny space where the laptop sat.

Sharma knew the time stamp from his own footage had Alexander Mathison stepping into Buenos Tempos at 5:25pm, so he forwarded yesterday's footage to 5:25 and sure enough, Alexander Mathison walked through the door.

'That's so sad,' the woman murmured, looking over Sharma's shoulder.

Sharma also felt a twinge of emotion watching this man who would soon be dead. He couldn't help it, but he also had a job to do here and he wanted to return to the Incident Room with way more information than they currently had.

Sharma reversed the tape to find the moment that the woman walked into the restaurant. She arrived much earlier than Alexander Mathison, just after five o'clock and ordered a bottle of wine. Clearly she was anticipating a longer evening than just a quick drink. Sharma watched the woman pour herself a glass and then look out the window at what would have been a busy Friday evening. She didn't pull out a book or the paper to read and she only checked her phone a few times before placing it back on the table in front of her.

She's expecting him at any minute, Sharma thought. Or she is very comfortable waiting.

Sharma forwarded the tape to Alexander's arrival and then let it run. He greeted her with a peck on each cheek and sat down. The woman poured him a glass of wine and they clinked glasses. She was leaning back in her chair. He was leaning slightly forward in his. Who was she?

Come on, Sharma silently urged the footage, show us something else.

It didn't take long.

Alexander Mathison reached forward and brushed a lock of the woman's hair back off of her face. The woman was very still, but Sharma could see that she was laughing. Alexander threw his arms out in gesture that Sharma couldn't quite interpret without the accompanying soundtrack of a conversation. It could have been to emphasize something, it could have been a gesture in mock surrender, or it could have been an exclamation. Whatever it was, Alexander moved his hands forward and pulled the woman towards him. The kiss filled in the gap.

'Oh my god,' said the woman. 'His girlfriend must be devastated.'

Sharma suddenly realized his error. He should never have let this employee look over his shoulder at the footage. What if this got out? What if the woman went to the press? Sharma was deeply out of his depth here and felt a bit sick. He needed Lombardi and he needed her now.

'I'm not sure any of this is actually relevant to the case,' he said abruptly. 'But thank you very much for showing me. I'll need all of the login details and we'll go through it one further time at the station.'

'Sure,' the woman said, clueless to Sharma's sudden panic.

Lombardi appeared at the door to the back office, the look on her face the polar opposite to the one on Sharma's.

'I've got it,' she said. 'Do you have the footage?'

'Yes,' Sharma said, clearing his throat. 'We can go.'

Thanking the staff, Lombardi and Sharma headed back towards the car.

'What do you have?' he finally asked.

'The receipt. She paid. Her name is Jennifer Clunes. Definitely not his wife.'

'Oh definitely not,' Sharma replied.

Twenty-Two

Luke and Hana had parked around the corner from the Mathison residence and were taking a moment to go through everything they had so far, which wasn't a hell of a lot. They knew this was going to be a difficult interview, but at least they would get the chance to rectify not having visited the woman the night before to tell her that her husband was dead.

Death was hard enough. Murder was infinitely more difficult.

'How do you want to handle this?' Hana asked.

'I'm actually not sure,' Luke said. 'We're dealing with someone who is absolutely depraved, Hana. Those notes were fucking sinister.'

'I know.'

'I mean this guy must really hate these people to kill them like this. And right now I'm not seeing the connection. So we're going to have to try to get a sense of one right now.'

'What if they're not connected?'

Luke took a deep breath.

'I don't even want to think about that. There's going to be one. There always is.'

The two detectives made their way down the street and around to Alexander and Amelia Mathison's house. The support officers were not in a marked police car, providing this grieving woman the same privacy and courtesy from the prying eyes of neighbours that Luke and Hana were trying to give by parking on the adjacent road.

The house was semi-detached, a small two storey property. Once upon a time this area had been considered on the rough side, but when the artists moved in and set up their studios, it became cool. The restaurants and shops followed that and now you'd need a hefty salary to afford the kind of mortgage that probably came with this house.

'Not too far from you here,' Luke said.

'This is the right postcode still though,' Hana said. 'Mine's not.'

'Right.'

'Your postcode actually has a dollar sign in front of it,' Hana said.

Luke pursed his lips and squinted at her, as if to say: *very funny.*

He lifted the knocker on the front of the door and gently tapped it a couple of times. The door opened to a support officer they both knew, Luke suddenly relieved that the woman who lived here was being well looked after.

'DCI Wiley, DS Sawatsky, lovely to see you. Sorry about the circumstances.'

'Hi,' Luke said. 'How is everyone doing?'

'We're through here. I'm just about to make some tea. What can I get you?'

Luke and Hana both declined the offer, still a little too full of the coffee they had consumed in the Incident Room.

The house was tidy and well decorated, lots of neutral

tones and soft furnishings. It was a comfortable home, and walking through it towards the kitchen, it was clear that no children lived here. The detectives both felt relieved by this.

Amelia Mathison was sitting at the long table in the centre of the kitchen, a bench on either side of it. It was the kind of table that would have fit well in a farmhouse kitchen, not in the centre of London.

She was mid-thirties, petite, with a round face and blonde hair that was cut into a bob. Her fringe hung limply across her forehead, as if she had been pushing it away from her face constantly, making the hair greasy. She looked absolutely exhausted, her eyes bloodshot from tiredness or crying or probably both.

'Amelia? My name is Hana Sawatsky. I am the detective sargeant working on your husband's case and this is my partner, detective chief inspector Luke Wiley.'

Amelia looked at them and nodded, but didn't say anything.

Luke pulled the bench opposite to Amelia out from under the table and swung his legs over it, sitting down. Hana joined him.

'We cannot express how sorry we are for your loss, Mrs. Mathison,' Luke said.

'Thank you,' the woman said with a politeness that must have been excruciating for her. 'Please call me Amelia.'

'I can't imagine how much of a shock this all is,' said Hana.

Amelia didn't answer or nod or look at Hana as she was spoken to. She was clearly still in shock and Hana wondered how much they were going to get out of her on this first visit. Figuring it was best to stick to easy facts, she tried again.

'You were in Suffolk last night?'

'Yes, we have a second home there.'

'How nice,' Hana said.

'When did you arrive there, Amelia?' Luke asked.

'I went out on Thursday late afternoon. I don't work in the office on Fridays, so I thought I'd have the day out there on my own. I like doing that when I can. Tidying up, doing some cooking, and then Alex comes and joins me when he is finished work on a Friday.'

'Did you drive out to Suffolk?' Luke asked.

'No, I took the train and then a taxi from the station. We don't really use our car in London very much so we tend to keep it in the country unless we know we need to be driving a lot of stuff back and forth.'

It seemed like a random question, but Hana could see that Luke was using answers the grieving woman would be able to answer easily, and then use these to try to build a picture of what their normal day-to-day life looked like. Something in that normal life was unusual, and they had to find it.

'What time did you expect your husband to be home last night?'

'Just after eight o'clock.'

'Did you speak to him in the hour or so before his train?' Luke asked.

Amelia shook her head.

'No, I spoke to him earlier in the afternoon. But not after that.'

As she said this, the tears began and Amelia clutched the side of the table, the realization that she wouldn't ever speak to him again written starkly across her face.

Luke and Hana knew that this detail was important. Alexander Mathison didn't make the six thirty train, but he clearly didn't call his wife to tell her this. Why not?

'Is the six thirty train the one he usually gets on a Friday?' said Hana.

'Most often, yes. Sometimes I meet him at the station if we go up together.'

'I'm sorry, I don't understand why you are asking me all of these questions,' said Amelia. 'I came back to London because I want to get to my husband. When can I see him?'

Her eyes were pleading, desperate. Luke understood these eyes and what they meant. He pushed away his own emotion which he could feel rising in his chest. This poor woman, her entire life and the future that she thought she had completely disappeared in an instant. Very soon, Luke knew, when the shock wore off a bit, she would feel desperate all over again in a different way when she realized that she didn't know what to do. She would despair at even the idea of a different life. It would feel impossible.

'We can arrange this for you later this afternoon. It's not a problem at all. The support officers will assist with everything and take you there,' Luke said.

The officer standing at the kitchen counter, brewing a pot of tea nodded at Luke as if to say that everything was in hand.

'I'm sorry that we have to go through a few of these things right now,' Luke continued. 'We just need to get the best picture possible of what happened last night and why this has happened to your husband.'

At this comment, Amelia's head snapped up and her eyes looked wild.

'What do you mean why this happened? Someone shot a loaded gun in the middle of a busy train station and my husband was hit.'

Luke was dreading the next words that were about to come out of his mouth. If he had turned to look at Hana, he would have seen that she closed her eyes briefly, knowing what was coming.

'Amelia, this could have been what happened. That it was a terrible, unfortunate accident and that your husband was tragically in the wrong place at the wrong time,' Luke paused.

'But we also need to rule out that your husband was not the intended victim.'

There was another pause as Amelia Mathison took this in.

'What?' she finally whispered.

'This may absolutely not be the case, but we have a lot more information to gather before we can determine exactly what happened.'

The support officer put a mug of steaming tea in front of Amelia, who didn't seem to notice. The possibility that her husband was murdered was not something that she seemed to be able to take in. This wasn't particularly helpful to Luke and Hana. It looked like an honest reaction, which meant that if Alexander Mathison was involved in something that got him killed, his wife certainly didn't know about it.

'Amelia,' Hana said gently. 'We have not released your husband's name and don't need to do so yet. You may want to think about who may need to know that your husband has died before the media receives this information. The support officers will help you with this.'

'Okay,' Amelia said, looking dazed.

Luke's phone began to vibrate in his pocket and he quickly pulled it out to see who was ringing him. It was O'Donnell, so he silenced the vibration and put the phone back in his pocket. Stephen O'Donnell could wait.

Hana's phone was on the table and she glanced down at it. She saw the text that had flashed up on her screen from Rowdy.

She slid the phone across the table so it was in front of Luke. He read the text and looked at her.

'Excuse me for a moment,' he said, standing up and moving into the other room.

The text was just four words.

Victim shot. Hyde Park.

TWENTY-THREE

Hyde Park was completely sealed off. Traffic had been stopped from entering from any road, which was the easiest part of the exercise as the park was shut to traffic every Sunday and the protocols were simple to enact. What was much more difficult was trying to shepherd hundreds of people out of 350 acres. When Luke arrived and was waved through towards the Serpentine Gallery which he was told was the closest parking place to where the victim was shot, he saw the officers fanning out across the green expanse and wondered why they were even bothering to try.

It would have been O'Donnell who had thought that closing the entire park to people was the appropriate use of police power.

Jesus, Luke thought as he began to walk across the fields towards the tree line. He had left Hana with Amelia Mathison to see if any other information could be pulled out of her, but Luke thought this was probably unlikely. At least O'Donnell would be less irritated to just see Luke approaching the scene instead of both of them.

The fact that Luke couldn't see any police from his

vantage point wasn't ideal. Assuming the victim had been shot where the body was found, no one from this side of the park would have seen a thing.

Hyde Park was something that as a Londoner you were always aware of, its central prominence in the heart of the city, but you never really got a sense of its size and scale until you were in it. It was vast and Luke noticed how, even with a huge police presence, he wasn't encountering anyone as he hurried towards the scene. He had been walking for a good six or seven minutes until he finally crested over a slight hill and saw the tenting going up by the forensics team who had reached the victim.

There were three people standing to one side of the plastic sheeting. One was O'Donnell, one was Dr. Chung, and the other was a woman he did not recognize. As he approached them, cursing his footwear which was not made for trekking through a muddy park in winter, he slowed down to take in the three of them. The dynamic between them was not as he would have expected. O'Donnell wasn't trying to tower over the two women, a difficult feat at any time due to his stature. He probably thought he was over six feet but was in reality nowhere close to it. His chest wasn't puffed out and he wasn't barking at them, or indeed at anyone else around them. He looked — could it be — anxious?

O'Donnell also looked like he was receiving a lecture, or at the very least, instructions from the woman that Luke did not know. Luke wondered what the hell was going on and why his boss didn't seem to be in charge. Not many people outranked the Superintendent.

O'Donnell caught sight of Luke walking towards them and stepped back from Dr. Chung and the other woman. He nodded at the two women and began to stride towards Luke.

Shit. This couldn't be good.

'Wiley!'

'Sir.'

'Where is Sawatsky?' O'Donnell said.

'With Amelia Mathison. Trying to figure out the last movements of the husband last night.'

O'Donnell looked back over his shoulder, as if we was worried he was being watched. But he wasn't. Dr. Chung and the other woman had moved behind the sheeting, closer to the body.

'Do we know what has happened, Sir?' Luke asked.

'It's fucking serious, Wiley. Another person has been shot. A man, looks to be in his early fifties. No ID yet. Shot in the back of the head. Executed. Just like the others.'

Luke took a deep breath, realizing that he had been holding it as O'Donnell was speaking, bracing for the details.

'Witnesses?'

'Absolutely no one. How is that possible? It's central London for godssake,' O'Donnell said.

'Media are gathering, Sir. They managed to get up past the Serpentine. Reports of the shooting were on the radio as I drove over here.'

'We can't have panic,' said O'Donnell, as Luke thought that was exactly what he was doing.

'Shall we see what we're dealing with and then provide a short statement to them to try to calm things down a bit?'

'Fine.'

'Sir, who is with Dr. Chung?' Luke asked as he began to walk towards the body and join the others.

'Wiley,' O'Donnell said. It was an instruction to stop moving. Luke understood and stepped back and leaned towards his boss, wondering what the hell was going on.

'She's MI5.'

Luke took a moment to take in what O'Donnell had said.

'Is there something else going on that we don't know about?' Luke asked.

O'Donnell shook his head.

'I honestly don't know. But she was called in from above.'

'From...' Luke said, just as he saw another woman striding towards them across the field, flanked by officers on each side of her. This woman was very familiar to Luke and he smiled as he watched her approach.

O'Donnell turned around to see what had caused Luke to stop mid-sentence. If Luke had been in a poor choice of footwear, this woman was in another category of poor footwear choices altogether.

Luke and O'Donnell were both slightly transfixed, watching her move towards them, seemingly unfazed by having to stop briefly every few steps to yank her foot out of the sludge she was sinking into.

'She's still in heels,' O'Donnell said.

'To be fair, Sir, I believe they are boots. With heels,' Luke replied.

O'Donnell snapped out of whatever sort of trance he had fallen into watching her approach and jumped to attention. He made a beeline for her, like a fevered teenager running after their favourite pop star .

She didn't stop for him, but kept moving towards Luke, turning her head every now and then to listen to what O'Donnell was saying.

This was going to be interesting.

Marina Scott-Carson was rarely seen outside of Scotland Yard by anyone who worked there. As the Commissioner, her office was on the top floor and most people knew she was up there, but only saw her as she walked through the building. She probably spent quite a bit of time outside of Scotland Yard, but eating in the kind of private member clubs that were above everyone's pay grade and social pedigree. Hana liked to tease Luke that he was the only person who had ever been in her office, and that was because she had a particular, inappropriate affection for him.

She did like Luke and was the main reason he had been allowed to come back to work after the disastrous Marcus Wright case. Without her approval, O'Donnell would never have given the go-ahead for Luke to return and to re-partner with Hana. But why Scott-Carson liked Luke he wasn't really sure. His case results were good, and she needed those numbers. But on the other hand, she kept Stephen O'Donnell around and in charge of the Serious Crime Unit and he was completely useless. She certainly wouldn't be threatened that O'Donnell was going to take her job.

Luke had always liked Marina Scott-Carson, and he respected her. He wasn't even remotely intimidated by her and he thought that this would have put her off. He could tell that she relished being at this level of power. Who the hell else would walk across the muddy fields of Hyde Park in a pair of high heeled boots and not think that she looked ridiculous?

Luke waited for this unlikely pair and Scott-Carson stopped when they reached him.

'Afternoon, Marina,' he said.

Marina Scott-Carson sighed and pursed her lips at the same time. Luke just nodded at her, the understanding between them that what they were about to encounter wasn't going to be pretty.

'Talk me through it, DCI Wiley.'

'Your guess is as good as mine at this point,' Luke said. 'I just got here.'

'Well then, detective. Shall we?'

Scott-Carson gestured for O'Donnell to head on towards the activity in front of them and he scurried to attention and up towards the trees. Luke and Scott-Carson followed behind O'Donnell and just before they reached the plastic sheeting and the array of officers assessing and marking off the scene, she grabbed Luke's arm and pulled him towards her.

Realizing that she was waiting to whisper something in his ear, Luke stooped down a bit and leaned in.

Whispering, she said, 'Will you please find me a goddamn pair of wellies?'

TWENTY-FOUR

They had yet to move the body.

This actually did not happen very often when Luke was summoned to a crime scene. Usually the body had been moved for an examination, or there had been an attempted resuscitation, or the body was no longer there at all.

Even for Luke, who had seen it all, this was a shock to witness.

A man had been executed in plain sight, in daylight, in the middle of Hyde Park.

It was almost as if the man had decided to gently lie down and close his eyes for a moment. He lay on his side, his legs folded up into his body just slightly. One arm Luke couldn't see as it was tucked underneath the rest of the body. The other was outstretched, its hand limp and already white from lack of blood flow and the cold temperature outside. Looking at it made Luke wish he had brought his gloves, his own hands suddenly feeling stiff and painful and his tucked one of them under the opposite armpit as he stared at the victim.

If you had come across this man while walking through

the park, your first assumption would be that he had lay down to rest for some strange reason.

Until you saw the back of his head.

Luke's immediate reflex was to swallow, the saliva involuntarily flooding into his mouth. He hadn't experienced this reaction in some time and shook his head to shake off the unwelcome wave of nausea that he knew was about to come.

The back of the man's skull had been blown open by the bullet and the tangle of bloodied hair, skull bone and brain matter was a gruesome mess.

'Jesus,' said Marina Scott-Carson.

Dr. Chung stood staring at the body with the rest of them and she wiped her fringe off her forehead with her arm, her hand still inside the latex gloves she had put on to examine the body. Luke noticed that she was sweating, her fringe sticking up in odd angles from her head.

Dr. Chung never displayed any kind of stress in all of the years Luke had worked with her. To see her sweating, especially in this cold weather, was indicative of how serious this situation was becoming. And fast.

'He was crouched down, facing the ground when he was shot,' Dr. Chung said.

She moved around the body and pointed to his head.

'I can already see through the mud on his forehead that a contusion is forming. He went straight down onto the front of his face. I wouldn't even be surprised if his nose is broken when we get him back to the lab and I take a closer look.'

Luke moved around to join Dr. Chung in front of the victim, partly to take a look and partly to help quell his rising nausea.

'And obviously he was shot in the back of the head,' Dr. Chung continued. 'But from the angle of the entry wound, the killer was standing above him.'

'Could the killer have been quite tall and that has affected the entry wound?' Scott-Carson asked.

'I'm not going to be able to determine height,' Dr. Chung said. 'But the killer would have had to be twelve feet tall to have achieved this angle if the victim had been standing when he was shot.'

'Do we have an ID yet?' Luke asked.

'No one has touched him,' Dr. Chung said.

Luke understood why. Whoever came across this poor soul lying on the ground like this would have seen the back half of his skull missing and likely gone into shock. The call to emergency services would have been quick and possibly hysterical. The responding police officer would not have touched him and any emergency medical team wouldn't have even tried to help the man.

'Who called this in?' Luke asked.

'It was a young woman on a run. We've called for victim support for her. We have her statement but she has already been taken home,' O'Donnell said.

'Is that wise?'

Finally, the woman who had been completely silent, taking everything in but giving nothing in return, had spoken.

Luke had tried not to pay too much attention to her when he got to the body. His instinct was not to give someone from MI5 much in terms of deference. He was the DCI on this case and he wished to remain so. He also wasn't in the habit of immediately trusting someone who had been thrust upon a scene that shouldn't necessarily be there.

'Meaning?' O'Donnell said. Where Luke was slightly wary of this new person, O'Donnell's reaction was predictably one of immense irritation.

'Four people have been shot in three days. Three of these four people are dead. The media are about to have a field day with this. We could at least hold back the details of this partic-

ular death so as not to stoke panic, which is about to be
inevitable. But you have just let the only member of the public
who has seen the state of this poor man go home to pick up
the phone and call everyone she knows. I'm going to say that
was not particularly wise. What do you think?'

O'Donnell opened his mouth but seemed unable to say
anything in return. Luke almost felt sorry for him. For a
nanosecond.

'Good afternoon,' the woman said, turning to Luke. 'My
apologies for not introducing myself.'

She stepped around the body and took two long strides
towards Luke so she was right in front of him. She was tall,
Luke guessed around five foot ten, and the second thing he
noticed as he was standing so close to him, was her incredible
cheekbones framed by long chestnut brown hair. She looked
to be around his own age, early forties, or possibly even a bit
younger. She was very striking and Luke wondered if this gave
her an air of seniority on the scene, or if she was just supremely
confident.

The woman extended her hand.

'Fiona Holland,' she said.

Luke shook her hand, feeling the slight calluses on her
palm. She did some kind of manual work to get those, he
thought. He was intrigued, as the clothes that he could see
under her long, belted wool coat seemed to be a pair of beauti-
fully tailored trousers. He looked down quickly and saw a pair
of sturdy, ankle length Barbour boots. This woman looked like
she would be comfortable in the company of Marina Scott-
Carson, even though she would be about twenty years
younger.

'Luke Wiley.'

'Wiley is the DCI on the Serious Crime Unit at the Met,'
Scott-Carson said.

'I know who he is,' said Fiona.

Luke wasn't sure what to make of that comment, so he reached into his pocket and took out a pair of latex gloves, pulling them onto his hands. Better to get stuck in and be useful than to continue with this strange show of posturing. Fiona Holland hadn't said that she was MI5 and Luke certainly wasn't going to ask who she worked with. Or who she worked for.

'Dr. Chung, have all of the photographs been taken?' Luke asked, nodding towards the victim.

'Yes, go ahead but try not to move him. I don't want that wound interfered with before I get him back to the lab. I'm going to instruct that he is transported face down.'

Everyone grimaced as Dr. Chung said this. Practical, as always, she tried to explain.

'We're going to need to determine what kind of gun was used — although I'd guess right now that it was the same large barrelled revolver — and I don't see an exit wound.'

'Oh Christ,' O'Donnell said.

'Understood,' Luke nodded to Dr. Chung, and crouched down next to the victim.

He took a good look at the man's clothing before doing anything else. He had been dressed for the weather — boots, a warm jacket that looked like a ski jacket — but he had on a pair of lined track suit bottoms, the kind that you would wear running in inclement weather. But the man hadn't been running. Just out for a walk maybe?

The track suit bottoms made it a bit easier for Luke to pat down both sides where the pockets sat. One side was flat and empty, but the other had a soft lump in it. Luke gently pulled out the pocket's content and revealed a fleece glove. Just one glove.

He held it up and Dr. Chung was the only one who understood what he needed and brought him an evidence bag so he could drop it inside.

'I'm going to guess that when we do lift him, the other hand that's underneath him still has its glove on,' Luke said. 'And he's wearing boots without laces, so he wasn't bent down tying anything.'

Luke needed to get even lower to try to determine if there were other pockets in the man's jacket that he could access without moving him too much. His knees sank slightly into the cold earth, the cold of the ground seeping into them very quickly. Luke rocked back and shifted his weight onto his heels and stood up.

'We're going to need to lift him, I'm afraid.'

Dr. Chung nodded and beckoned over a couple of her colleagues, who were standing to the side, diligently watching the detectives work.

They worked quickly, accustomed to the dead weight of a body such as this one, understanding the movements and rhythm of moving it with ease. They rolled out the thick rubber sheeting, unfurling the handles that lay on both sides of it, next to the man. On a count of three they eased him upwards to the right, shifted the rubber underneath him and then repeated the movement on the lefthand side.

'Wait, please,' Luke said as he moved into position next to the body so he was ready for their next movement as they adjusted the body on the sheet. As they lifted the body again, Luke pulled both sides of the man's jacket outwards, unzipping it as best he could, freeing the fabric shell on both sides. He quickly patted down the man's chest, but could feel nothing there.

'Okay, thank you,' he said.

The man's jacket pockets did not reveal very much. A carefully folded tissue, a few pound coins, a set of house keys. There was no wallet, no bank card, no mobile phone.

This man had either been robbed or had just popped out

of the house momentarily. But why was he in the middle of Hyde Park? And why kill him?

As Luke stood up, he scanned the horizon, looking for the missing piece of this puzzle, suddenly realizing what it must be. He looked at Fiona Holland who had already stepped away from the group, looking out across the park for the same thing.

TWENTY-FIVE

The decision had been made to brief the media.

Fiona Holland had been spot on with her evaluation of what was going to happen next. Three people shot to death in central London, another victim still in hospital. The public would begin to panic. The papers would stoke it to sell more copies, to go for more advertising clicks on their websites.

Fiona and Luke had left the others at the scene and they would leave the park from the north side on Bayswater, away from where the media cameras had gathered. Luke would give a short statement, away from the big bosses so that the scene in Hyde Park wouldn't look to have any more importance than a simple, unexplained death. The sight of Marina Scott-Carson would have sent the journalists into a frenzy.

'I'm told that the media get on quite well with you,' Fiona said as she and Luke walked down towards the Serpentine.

'I'm not sure who told you that, but it's a rather kind and misguided appraisal.'

'They don't like you then?'

'Are you universally liked, Ms. Holland?'

Luke could just see Fiona smiling out of the corner of his eye.

'Oh certainly not,' she said.

Luke wondered why this woman was at the scene and had so many questions to ask her. He thought he may as well get straight to the point if they had any chance of figuring out what the hell was going on.

'Why is MI5 on this?' Luke asked.

'We're across most things you do,' Fiona replied.

'What me specifically, or the entire Metropolitan Police Force?'

'Just you,' she whipped back.

Luke stopped and couldn't help but smile himself. It was a bit of a balm after the past hour examining the shattered skull of the dead man.

Fiona did not stop, but kept striding ahead of him. Luke wondered for a moment if she wanted him to watch her from behind. He took a deep breath.

'Are you coming?' she shouted back at him.

He found his tongue had jabbed into the inside of his cheek, something he sometimes did when he was nervous, or amused, or just a little bit pleased but didn't wish to show it. Luke began moving again and joined her, slipping a bit as he did so. The grass had become very muddy in this stretch of the park and even with boots on they were treading carefully.

'Really,' he said. 'What's going on? I can't do my job properly if you are withholding information.'

Fiona finally turned towards Luke and looked bemused.

'I'm MI5,' she said. 'All we do is withhold information.'

Luke took a moment to figure out his next move, like he was playing a game of chess. Fiona Holland was clearly good at her job. But before he could ask another question, she finally threw him a bone.

'We had to get involved,' Fiona said. 'It's nothing personal.

The first two shootings could be connected, but we were advised by Marina that this may not be the case.'

Luke raised his eyebrows at this comment, wondering how closely Marina Scott-Carson was actually watching them. Or watching Luke specifically.

'Shootings are rare in London if they aren't gang related, and these don't appear to be so. Could be some sort of initiation, but again we aren't seeing that on our Gang Taskforce. If there is even the slightest whiff that the shootings could be terrorist related, we are involved.'

'Is that your analysis at the moment?' Luke asked.

'That it's terrorist-related? Not particularly. But after this morning, if someone is going around picking off members of the public with some sort of grievance, then I'm going to change my mind.'

Luke agreed with her, and if he didn't already feel like he was two steps behind the killer, he certainly felt so at this moment, in the middle of this conversation.

'Are you clear about what you're going to say to our friends?' Fiona asked, staring ahead at the line of officers who were holding back a throng of cameramen, journalists and at least a hundred members of the public, standing behind them all craning their necks upwards to try to catch a glimpse of why the park was shut.

'They are going to ask if this death is related to the two other shootings,' Luke said.

'Well, that's an easy answer. They are not. And as we don't exactly know whether they are or aren't at this point, you should be able to say that with a clear conscience.'

'Is there anything you would like me to say specifically about the previous shootings?'

Fiona stopped and crossed her arms. Luke paused as well and waited for her answer.

'What do you think has happened, DCI Wiley? Before we get to the media scrum, before we go back to Scotland Yard, I'd like your view, please.'

Luke respected that she was asking this. He had spent years working with bosses who were only interested in their own viewpoint.

'There is still a possibility that these are connected,' Luke said. 'Both men who have been killed — Trevor Alpine in the wine bar by the British Museum and Alexander Mathison in Liverpool Street Station were both lawyers. It could be a disgruntled client. When we ID the body in the park, if he's a lawyer, then I'll be convinced of this.'

'They worked at different law firms,' Fiona said.

Luke realized with this comment that Fiona Holland was completely up to speed on this investigation and he wondered when exactly she had been briefed. And by whom.

'Yes, they did. My colleagues are going through their client lists to see if anyone appears on both,' Luke said.

'And the woman in the wine bar? The date? Was she in the wrong place at the wrong time?'

'Possibly,' Luke said. 'But she has an ex-husband who has just appeared out of nowhere the second she began dating Trevor Alpine. We're looking into it.'

'And this would be connected with Alexander Mathison how?' Fiona asked.

'We're on it,' Luke said, hoping that he sounded more convincing than he felt.

"Well then,' Fiona said, continuing to walk towards the crowd gathered on the road. 'I think you'll handle this little soundbite just fine. The briefer the better, DCI Wiley. Oh, and feel free to call me Fiona.'

Before he could reply, Fiona peeled off to the left and away from the prying eyes of the journalists, leaving Luke to face them alone. He could see her standing to the side, still observing him when he reached the road.

Luke decided to go with the transparent, helpful approach, instead of a formal press conference. He smiled at everyone to try to seem reassuring, but hoped that his face didn't appear too relaxed because when the news emerged of what had actually occurred on the north side of Hyde Park this morning, he did not want the public to think they were not taking it as seriously as they were.

Christ I hope I'm getting this balance right, he thought.

Luke explained that the body of a man had been discovered by a member of the public earlier that morning and next of kin were being notified.

That was the first lie, as they still had no idea who was lying on the grass with the back of his head blown off.

No, Luke had said, they did not at this time believe there was any connection with the deaths by the British Museum and at Liverpool Street Station.

Lie number two.

The questions were coming thick and fast, being shouted out in rapid succession by so many people that it made the situation slightly easier for Luke. He wasn't calling on anyone individually, because this wasn't a proper press conference, and he could pretend that he was answering a question directly because god knows no one else could hear exactly what was being said either.

But then as Luke was thanking everyone for coming but intimating that they were all wasting their time on a nice sunny Saturday when they could be elsewhere, a question he had heard previously was shouted out in a moment of quiet and there was no way he was going to be able to avoid it.

'Was the man shot, detective?'

Luke wanted to look down at his feet, but forced himself to stare straight into the camera that was fixed upon him.

'We are still determining the cause of death and will release that information as soon as we have it. Thank you.'

The third lie was sticking in his throat and Luke walked back towards the scene and where he had parked his car. Fiona Holland was still standing there, looking down at her mobile phone. Luke didn't feel like speaking to her right now, he desperately wanted to shake off the feelings of unease at his obfuscation.

His own phone began to ring, and he felt relieved to have been given a reason to be occupied as he walked past her. It was O'Donnell calling him.

Swiping right to answer, Luke thought he'd circumvent any questions about the journalists for now — the Super would be able to watch the footage back eventually.

'It went well, Stephen. Nothing to worry about just yet,' Luke said.

'There is, Wiley. We have a big problem,' O'Donnell said.

As he explained what had happened and barked instructions that Luke didn't bother to listen to, Luke was already moving towards Fiona Holland and calling her name.

Fiona looked up and began to jog over to him.

'We need to get to the cafe on the Serpentine. It remained open and they've just discovered...'

'A dog,' Fiona said.

They stared at each other for a moment to take in that they had both come to the same conclusion back at the scene, but had said nothing, not wanting to send everyone on a wild goose chase for nothing. Or at least not yet.

'Yes,' said Luke.

'He had bent down to fix something on his dog's collar, perhaps reaffix the lead. He needed to have at least one glove off in order to be able to do it easily. As he was crouched down, he was shot in the back of the head.'

'Yes,' he said again.

'But how do they know this dog belongs to the victim?' Fiona asked.

Luke swallowed hard before answering.

'The collar,' he said. 'There's a note attached to it.'

Twenty-Six

D r. Nicky Bowman was having a quiet Saturday afternoon. She had spent much of the morning working, which was often what she did on a Saturday morning. While she enjoyed seeing her patients and sitting with them in conversation, listening to their thoughts and their difficulties and being present for them, she arguably enjoyed the work she did with them when they were not in the room.

Nicky did not take notes in her sessions — she couldn't listen properly if she was writing things down at the same time — but she scribbled a few key points and thoughts that she did not want to forget in the brief window she had between her patients. Then on a Saturday morning, she sat down again with the notes from her week and she went through them, thinking about her patients and filling in holes in her notes as she considered again the things that they had talked about. It felt almost like meditation, this continuation of a conversation that she had mostly with herself.

She tended to do this at the table in her dining room, which sat underneath the only skylight in the house. When it was sunny, the dining room table glittered in the light and when it rained as it so often did in London, it felt cozy and magical. As if she was sitting al fresco, but in the warmth and dry of her lovely home.

As Nicky lived alone, she often felt grateful that her dining room was part of a larger open plan space that incorporated both the small kitchen and then past the dining room and down a couple of steps was her living room. This, in turn, opened out onto a little garden and a deck that she used constantly in summertime. Had these rooms been separate, with doors that closed and radiators that needed to be turned on and off, she doubted that she would have used all of them. People who lived alone tended to gravitate towards one particular space in their home, she imagined. Hers was open and comfortable and she loved to be in it.

It had been a little late to be having caffeine — she never had it after 11am — but Nicky figured that as she didn't have to be up for a patient in the morning, she would brew another small pot of coffee and settle into her notes. She finished everything around 1pm and her stomach growled as if on cue.

She stood up and stretched and tidied up her notepad and file folders and stacked everything neatly on the side of the table to eventually be carried upstairs and put away properly in her office for the week's work ahead.

Nicky had planned to do a grocery shop later in the afternoon and figure out what to make for dinner then, so for lunch she pulled out a container of anchovies that had been marinating in olive oil and lemon juice and spooned them onto a piece of rye toast. Wiping her hands on a tea towel, she picked up one side of the toast she had sliced in half and took a bite as she moved into the living room and pressed the button on the remote to turn on the television.

The channel she had been watching the evening before flicked to life and predictably, it had been the twenty four hour news channel. What was it about watching the same news stories on a loop that was comforting? Perhaps it was particular to her personality — the tone of the newsreader, the channel's theme music, the short bursts of news that generally didn't affect your day to day life.

The first news story was one she had seen on this loop the previous day but the second story was new, the Breaking News banner displayed at the bottom of the screen.

'Oh my god,' Nicky said out loud.

It was Luke.

Fumbling for the remote control, she pressed the volume button and stopped chewing her piece of toast.

A dead body found in Hyde Park was not usually something that would be on the news in this way — it would be a smaller piece on the website, but this was a national newscast. Nicky was partly taking in the details, but mostly staring at her patient.

Luke was lying.

She could see it instantly.

The newscast was brief, less than two minutes long, and the channel moved onto another reporter. Nicky abandoned her lunch and headed upstairs to her office, forgetting to bring the neat stack of files on the dining table with her. In her office she didn't bother to sit down and opened her laptop, cursing that she had actually turned it off earlier that morning. As she waited for it to start up, she stared out of the window at the street below, thinking that she hadn't gone through any notes that morning for Luke because she hadn't seen him that week. It had been odd to get a call from him on a Saturday morning and for him to then text to tell her that he was home early from his holiday.

Something was going on.

Nicky pulled up the website for the news channel and scrolled down until she found the story. She clicked on the video and watched Luke again. He was doing what he did when he first turned up at her house a year and a half ago. His demeanour open and the words coming out of his mouth clear and calm. But his eyes betrayed him. They weren't sure where to focus, what to look at, moving side to side as if he was looking for an answer — one that was truthful, one that didn't match what he was saying out loud.

No one watching this newscast would likely know what was going on for Luke Wiley. The journalists assembled in front of him wouldn't know, the viewer at home wouldn't have a clue. Nicky wondered who else would really know that there was a different truth behind the words coming out of Luke's mouth. She imagined that his late wife would have known. Perhaps Hana would know. These two people who Nicky heard about all the time but had never met.

And Nicky knew this state of being extremely well. She saw it in her patients, of course, but she knew it on a very personal level.

There were many things that Luke did not know about his therapist. The relationship was always going to be one-sided. As much as Nicky liked Luke and would have felt comfortable with him knowing about various aspects of her life, it wouldn't be helpful for him. The therapeutic relationship required that she remain a blank slate. But as Luke sat on the sofa in her office and spoke about his wife, the grief being experienced by this man almost made Nicky change her mind. It was a privilege to witness such profound grief, that Luke allowed such a personal experience to be known by her. But it was sometimes excruciating to sit with it.

Because it was so close to her own.

It had been nine years since Nicky's husband had died.

Luke did not know this.

Her husband's death had been a shock. It wasn't as instant for her as it was for Luke — she did not receive a phone call or have her colleague turn up at her front door to tell her that Sean was dead. The MRI scan that was shown to Nicky and Sean in a cold, clinical hospital room revealed to them that he would be dead in a matter of weeks.

It had turned out to be nine weeks exactly.

So when Luke turned up at her front door, a completely broken man, Nicky had understood. This is why she never told him that his grief would subside or that time would heal. Because neither of these things would happen. She wasn't sure that this is why Luke opened up to her so quickly, but she suspected it may be the case.

His work as a detective could sniff out bullshit or a fake platitude a mile away. She was sure, at least, about that. She tried to be thorough, and thoughtful and empathetic in the work she did as a therapist, and she could see that her new patient approached his own job the same way.

But she had not told Luke about Sean.

So when Nicky saw her patient on the news, the look in his eyes and the text he had sent her earlier had her very concerned and she knew what she was going to do.

She picked up her mobile and found Luke's text from just hours before. She replied to it, saying that she was available today or tomorrow if he wanted to come over.

It took about an hour for Luke to respond, his text saying that the only time he would be available would be the next morning at 6am.

Nicky didn't have sessions with her patients at 6am and Luke knew this, yet he was suggesting it.

Nicky stared at her phone and knew that neither she nor Luke would probably be sleeping that night. She typed back a message.

I'll have the coffee ready.

Twenty-Seven

The cafe on the Serpentine was on the opposite side of the park from where the man was shot and killed. This section had been closed to cars, but not to the public who were on foot, although the cafe had since been closed and emptied of its patrons after the dog and the note had been discovered and officers had arrived on the scene.

Police had cordoned off the cafe and Fiona and Luke had been close enough to Luke's car that they had decided to drive over to the scene, which saved them about fifteen minutes of crossing the muddy park on foot.

The dog was a brown and black terrier, sitting very obediently with a staff member from the cafe, who was scratching behind his ears.

Shit, Luke thought, just as Fiona Holland shouted to the girl.

'Please don't touch the dog!'

The poor girl looked suddenly terrified and jumped up from her chair, raising her hands like she was being held at gunpoint.

'I'm sorry,' Fiona said. 'I didn't mean to frighten you.'

The girl welled up and nodded her head.

Luke was pulling on a pair of latex gloves while looking around the cafe, trying to determine who else was in there with them. He could see some kitchen staff behind the counter who had been allowed to remain behind. Two other cafe workers sat at a table to the side, chatting to each other.

'Who found the dog, please?'

'I did,' the girl said.

'What's your name, lovely?' Fiona asked, her tone considerably softened.

'Phoebe.'

'Phoebe,' Fiona said. 'It's really important that you tell me exactly what happened and what you saw. No detail is too small. You're not in any kind of trouble, so don't worry about that. We just really need to know everything because it's going to help us enormously. Okay?'

Phoebe nodded her head.

She had noticed the dog tied outside to the bike rack next to the door of the cafe sometime around 11am when she took her break. Luke looked at his watch and could see that it was now almost two o'clock.

Three hours was a lot of time to disappear.

When Phoebe went to clear and wipe down some tables at around noon, she noticed that the dog was still there. It seemed a bit of a long time to be tied up outside and she looked around the cafe, trying to determine which customer the dog may belong to. She was called away by the kitchen and forgot about it, but when it came time for Phoebe to take her lunch break and the dog was still outside, she went out to see him.

'And that's when you saw the note?' Luke asked.

'Yes. I thought at first that the dog had been abandoned

and that the note was a kind of 'I'm sorry but please look after my dog' note. Except it wasn't. I showed my friend who works with me here and he said I needed to call the police.'

'Which officer did you hand the note to?' Luke asked.

Phoebe pointed through the window to a short, stocky policeman and Fiona beckoned him inside. As she was dealing with the officer, Luke asked Phoebe if she had seen anyone unusual come in that morning, specifically any man of average height in a hoodie who was on his own.

She shook her head.

Luke looked up at the camera in the cafe and picked up his phone to call Sharma.

'Any luck at the Dog and Duck or at the tapas restaurant?' Luke said.

Sharma filled him in, the news that the shooter seemed to disappear into thin air after entering the pub was beginning to feel like a pattern. He had clearly done the same here, unless Sharma could find some better footage on the cafe CCTV.

'We'd better hope so,' Sharma said. 'There's no other good camera in that park. It's a complete dead zone.'

After hanging up, Luke looked down at the dog. His lead was hanging limply on the floor, and the dog didn't seem to want to run.

'Good boy,' Luke said.

With his gloved hand, Luke carefully picked up the end of the lead.

'Phoebe?' he called to the girl, who had rejoined her friend. 'This is the same lead that he was tied up with?'

'Yes.'

'Okay, thanks.'

Luke caught Fiona's eye through the glass and attempted to mime an evidence bag, like he was playing a game of charades. She nodded.

The dog whined slightly and rested his head on Luke's foot. Luke couldn't help but smile and bent down to give the little guy a reassuring pat. His eye caught something on the dog's fur and Luke's hand stopped in mid-air, hovering just above the dog's head.

It was dried blood.

'I'm sorry,' Luke whispered to the dog.

What the poor dog must have seen. It's amazing that the gunshot didn't have the dog sprinting a mile away from the scene — the sound must have been deafening. Wanting to stay with his person, the dog didn't leave. Did he stare at his person lying dead on the ground? Did he nudge the body with his nose and whine like he just did with Luke?

Did the killer calmly pull the lead out of the dead man's hand and lead the dog off towards the cafe? It would appear so.

'If only you could speak,' Luke whispered. 'You could tell us what happened.'

The sound of Fiona clearing her throat startled Luke and he jumped.

She was standing right next to him, having slipped back in the cafe, and was smiling at Luke with a sympathetic, yet slightly mocking look on her face.

'You wanted an evidence bag?'

'Thanks,' Luke said, quickly taking it from her outstretched hand and dropping the lead into it.

'If you're finished your conversation there, do you want to have a look at this?' Fiona said.

Luke clenched his jaw and looked right into Fiona's eyes, hoping this direct stare would perhaps improve his reputation at this precise moment.

'The note?'

'Yes,' said Fiona. 'The officer was quick thinking enough

to get a sterile plastic bag from the cafe kitchen, but I don't think it's going to help. Multiple people have handled this note now — I doubt we could even establish the chain of handlers.'

Fiona passed the bag to Luke, who noticed immediately that the note was on a different type of paper than the ones that had been posted to Henry MacAskill.

'What is it?' Fiona asked, noticing how Luke was handling the bag.

'The note — it's on a stiffer card than the others. Those were on basic printer paper. Was it attached to the collar by this hole at the top?'

'The officer said that it was — affixed with a twist tie from a rubbish bag.'

'He planned this.'

'It would appear so.'

'He looked for a dog walker specifically to murder?' Luke said.

'Look at the note, Wiley.'

Luke squinted through the bag at the card, which was about four inches by six inches and had been perfectly folded in half before a hole punch had been used on the top right hand corner.

Like a goddamn card that you tie around a Christmas present, Luke thought to himself.

A printer wasn't used this time. This note was handwritten, in neat, block letters with black ink.

DO I HAVE YOUR ATTENTION NOW?

HENRY WILL PRINT THE MESSAGE BELOW OR MORE WILL DIE

YOU WILL FEAR ME FOR THAT IS HOW YOU LEARN

STIPENDIUM PECCSTI MORS EST

'My Latin is a little rusty,' Luke said. 'Do you have any idea what that means?'

Fiona was already a step ahead of him and handed Luke her phone. The screen had the translation app on it with the Latin verse inputted into it. The English translation sat below its Latin equivalent.

The reward of sin is death.

Twenty-Eight

'He seems very obedient. But he's also covered in blood and grey matter. We're going to have to take him into the station.'

'I don't particularly like dogs,' Fiona said.

'Right,' Luke said. 'Give me a second.'

He stepped aside and pulled out his phone to call Rowdy.

'Rowdy, I need two things please. Get Henry MacAskill over there as soon as you can. We need to speak to him. And is Parker with you?'

'He is,' Rowdy replied.

'Does he like dogs?'

'Uh, just a moment.'

Luke could hear the muffled sounds of a conversation happening in Scotland Yard, which went on far longer than the yes or no answer his question required.

'It would seem,' said Rowdy, 'that Officer Parker loves dogs and has, in fact, had several of them over the course of his young life including a particularly special one called Patches when he was about ten years old.'

'Of course he did,' sighed Luke.

After giving instructions for Parker to collect the dog from the cafe in Hyde Park, Luke told Rowdy that they would soon be back and to assemble everyone, including Henry, in the Incident Room.

'Hana is with you, then?' Rowdy said.

'No.'

There was a pause.

'Then who is the "we" coming back here?' Rowdy asked.

Luke looked over his shoulder to make sure that Fiona couldn't hear him, but she was deep in conversation on her own phone.

'MI5 is here, Rowdy. She's coming back with me.'

'Understood.'

Rowdy did understand instantly the seriousness with which this shooting was being taken. She hung up from Luke and ushered Parker out the door.

Sometimes Rowdy relished the role she had at the Met and with the Serious Crime Team. She knew that they probably couldn't function without her, or at least they would function less well and work less quickly, which was not ideal for the types of crime they investigated. She did not have children of her own, and was well past the point of being able to do so, so she did not mind the motherly role she often found herself taking on at the unit.

But there were other times where she felt like she was herding cats and she could really do without it. In her last annual review with the Super, she had gently asked O'Donnell about the specific terms of early retirement. He had balked at even the suggestion and she had left it at that.

But watching Parker bound out the door like a puppy, in order to go and pick up a puppy, she could only take a deep breath and try to focus on the task ahead of her.

She had been offered her own office a few years ago and it was moments like this one where she wished she had taken up the offer. She knew it had been Luke who pushed for it, who insisted that she was too important to be sitting in a cubicle in the centre of the floor with a dozen other staff members. But she preferred to be in the thick of it and it allowed her to do her job better. If she was sequestered away somewhere where she could shut the door, how would she see and hear everything that was going on?

She also knew that Luke had a soft spot for her. And Rowdy had a serious soft spot for him. The death of Luke's wife had been a tragedy beyond words — the whole department had felt it — but Rowdy had taken it especially badly for some reason. She was devastated that something this awful could happen to someone this good. It was bizarre to feel it so intensely, when this is what happened to people on a daily basis in her line of work. All of these shattered lives that they could not put back together, but they could find justice to help them on their way.

Rowdy picked up the phone to call Henry MacAskill on his mobile. She wasn't entirely sure what she thought of Henry, but chalked this up to a general distrust of journalists. They were never particularly helpful to the Met and when she had to run interference so a specific story wasn't printed, or a quote wasn't attributed to an officer who had said something they shouldn't have, it distracted her from the job.

'Henry, it's Laura Rowdy.'

'Hi Laura. Is everything alright?'

Rowdy wasn't sure how to answer this. She didn't fully trust Henry to pass along any information without Luke's permission.

'I'm not entirely sure,' she said. 'But Luke has asked that you come into Serious Crime as soon as you can.'

'Yes. Something else has happened,' Henry replied.

'In Hyde Park, I'm sure you saw.'

'No, Laura. That's not what I meant. I was just about to

ring to say that I needed to come into the Met. I don't know why this is happening to me, but I think the shooter has sent me an email.'

Rowdy felt the hairs on her forearm tingle when she heard this.

'Get in here, Henry,' she said. 'And be careful.'

Henry didn't say anything in response, but Rowdy could tell that he had stayed on the line for a moment, pausing before hanging up the call.

She was shocked that she had said this, that she had warned Henry to be aware of danger. But she knew she was suddenly feeling a heightened sense of it — the possibility that someone else could be hurt or shot or killed without warning. She tried to shake off the feeling but it hung in the air like static electricity. Something you couldn't see, but was there to shock you when you were least expecting it.

Twenty-Nine

Hana had spent longer with Amelia Mathison than she would have liked. The poor woman was clearly still in shock and it took ages to be able to get any good information out of her. In the end, Hana wasn't sure she had obtained any useful details about her husband. After her experience earlier in the day with Trevor Alpine's colleague turning up unexpectedly at Trevor's flat, Hana made sure to ask Amelia about her husband's work friends. Did he spent a lot of time with anyone specifically? Who would she consider to be his closest allies at the office?

Amelia had looked baffled at many of these questions and Hana didn't think she was bluffing. Her assessment was that the woman didn't know much at all about her husband's work or simply had never been interested in it.

Hana knew Alexander Mathison's date of birth and it was nowhere near his birthday, so before she left Amelia, she had one last question for her.

'Is it any special date for you and your husband? An anniversary, anything like that?'

Amelia looked confused by the question.

'No. Our wedding anniversary is in July. Why?'

'No specific reason. I just thought I'd ask.'

Hana wondered if she sounded convincing as she left the woman in the good care of the support officers and stepped outside. Luke had taken the car when he'd received the call from Rowdy about the latest shooting so Lombardi and Sharma were sent to collect her.

She was annoyed that they weren't already waiting outside for her and she tried to calm down. Impatient at the best of times, Hana felt like she had just wasted an hour and a half with someone who hadn't been able to help their investigation in the way she would have hoped.

She called Luke's mobile and it went to voicemail after the first ring. He had declined the call. This didn't exactly help her mood.

A Met police car finally appeared at the bottom of the road and Hana walked out to meet them. Lombardi was driving, which amused her, and when the car stopped next to Hana, Hana stood at the side of the front passenger door and waited. It took Sharma a good second to understand what was happening and he quickly opened the door, unfastened his seatbelt and apologized.

'Sorry,' he said, shuffling out of the way and giving the front seat to Hana.

Sharma grabbed the handle of the back passenger door and yanked it. It didn't open and he stumbled backwards.

'Yeah,' Hana said. 'Back doors are locked.'

Lombardi fumbled with the buttons on her door, unfamiliar with what opened what and finally released the lock so Sharma could get in.

'Thanks.'

Lombardi went to put the gear into drive and hesitated.

'Sorry DS Sawatsky, would you like to drive?'

Hana smiled.

'No no, I'm fine. Why don't you pull over up here and update me before we head back to the unit.'

'Well, that's the thing,' said Sharma from the backseat. 'I think we need to make one stop first.'

At this comment, Hana swivelled in her seat and looked back at him.

'Something tells me that the pair of you did a good job.'

Lombardi and Sharma looked enormously relieved.

'I hope so, Ma'am,' Lombardi said. 'I think we've got something.'

Parked on the side of the street, Lombardi and Sharma filled Hana in on the Dog and Duck and their lack of success there.

'He just vanished into thin air?' Hana said.

'There is no working camera at that back door, just the rubbish collection bins and a side street that has exits both ways. It would have been easy for the shooter to slip away. We've already called in about the rubbish bins and Rowdy was sending someone over to go through them. Maybe the gun was dropped in there?'

'I doubt it,' Hana said to Sharma. 'Especially if our Hyde Park shooter is the same guy.'

'Oh, okay.'

'But we may find something,' she said. 'It was smart to call it in right away.

'And Buenos Tiempos where Alexander Mathison ate before he was shot? Did you have a good time?' Hana asked.

The joke was completely lost on Sharma and Lombardi — they were too eager to tell Hana what they had discovered.

Hana pulled her phone out to call Rowdy and get an address for Jennifer Clunes.

'Already done that,' Sharma said. She's not very far from here. Straight up Kingsland Road to Stoke Newington. I've mapped it. Should take us fifteen minutes.'

'You're positive about this?' Hana asked. 'Jennifer Clunes is the woman you saw on the CCTV with Alexander Mathison?'

'It had better be,' replied Lombardi. 'On the footage we saw, we watched her give him the bracelet.'

Hana was impressed with her colleagues, although slightly less than impressed with Lombardi's driving as they made their way north towards the address they had for Jennifer Clunes. She was signalling early and changing lanes carefully and clearly not wanting to do anything illegal.

'Lombardi,' said Hana. 'You're a police officer. You can speed. Let's get there today, shall we?'

'Yes, Ma'am.

The car lurched forward as Lombardi pressed her foot down on the gas.

Jesus, Hana thought, making a note to herself that she would be driving back to Scotland Yard after this.

It was, indeed, just fifteen minutes to the address Sharma had once Lombardi had picked up the pace. Except the address was a small organic grocery store on the main road.

'Pull over here,' Hana instructed, craning her neck to look through the car window at the building. 'I'm going to guess that it's the flat above. Let's see if there's a buzzer for upstairs.'

The three of them exited the car, Lombardi delighted to be able to park illegally once again. There was a buzzer for both the grocer and the flat above but before Hana pressed it, she turned to her young colleagues with some words of caution.

'This is delicate and god forbid that we're wrong here. We also have not released Alexander Mathison's name publicly, so no mention of it. Let me do the talking. Understood?'

Lombardi and Sharma both nodded, relieved to be simply observing this time.

Hana pressed the buzzer and waited.

'Hello?' said a woman's voice.

'Is this Jennifer Clunes?'

'Yes.'

'My name is Detective Sargeant Hana Sawatsky from the Metropolitan Police. Could you come downstairs and speak to me for a moment?'

There was silence and the buzzer had not been pressed again to provide a reply. Hana strained to hear if there was any sound coming from the intercom. But it was only a matter of seconds before the front door to the street flung open and a woman was standing there in yoga pants and a jumper.

Hana could tell immediately that the woman knew exactly why they were there and that she was on the verge of becoming hysterical.

Hana could not risk a scene on a busy street, so she said just one thing to the woman, as gently as she could.

'Yes, we are here about Alexander Mathison.'

The woman suddenly looked like her legs were about to give way and she clutched the side of the door she had just opened.

'Let's go inside, Jennifer,' Hana said. 'I'll explain everything upstairs.'

Jennifer nodded and turned around to head back upstairs, clearly not thinking about the open door or the busy street past it. Hana followed her and motioned for the others to come inside and ensure that the door was shut and locked behind them.

When they reached the flat at the top of the stairs, Jennifer immediately went to sit down on her sofa, and stared up at the three of them. Hana realized that she had been assuming the worst for almost twenty four hours now.

'This is Officer Lombardi and Officer Sharma,' Hana said. 'They work with me.'

Jennifer didn't seem to take any of this in.

'He's dead, isn't he? It was Alex who was killed last night at Liverpool Street?'

'Yes, it was. I'm very sorry,' Hana said.

'Oh my god, oh my god.'

Jennifer clutched the front of her calves and began to rock back and forth on the sofa. Instinctively, Lombardi went and sat next to her on her right. She didn't touch Jennifer, but she leaned forward as if to offer a shoulder to lean into. It was a generous, spontaneous act of compassion and Hana smiled at her.

Lombardi only nodded.

'I knew it, I just knew it,' Jennifer said.

Hana was worried that Jennifer's state of shock was going to spiral into something that was difficult to manage.

'Sharma,' she instructed. 'Please find the kitchen and get Jennifer a glass of water.'

'Of course,' Sharma said and jumped up.

'Jennifer, I am so sorry. But it's important that I ask you a series of questions that I appreciate you won't feel like answering right now. We need to figure out who did this and we think you can help.'

'Oh my god, did Amelia tell you where to find me?'

'No,' said Hana. 'She did not mention you when I spoke to her earlier today.'

Jennifer's eyes widened and Hana could tell that she couldn't put the pieces together.

'We have you on CCTV at Buenos Tiempos last night with Alexander. You paid for the drinks. That's how we found you — the address is registered with your bank card.'

'Oh, okay,' Jennifer said, looking incredibly relieved. Hana thought that whether the wife knew or not was suddenly not going to matter to Jennifer when she fully took in that her lover was dead. Her brain had not caught up to the reality of what had happened, still functioning in the realm of secrecy and clandestine meetings.

'How long have you been having an affair?' Hana asked.

The relief with which Jennifer spoke as she explained the details of her affair with Alexander Mathison made Hana realize that this woman had not told anyone else about it. It was almost as if Hana was a close girlfriend that she was gossiping with — the person that you gushed your feelings to over a glass of wine and discussing the details of the relationship. Except, of course, Hana wasn't responding in kind and the weight of Jennifer's grief seemed to fill the room.

She was completely alone with the scale of this tragedy and this personal loss.

Lombardi and Sharma, silent and observing, felt enormously sorry for her, which was a rather stark change of opinion from their initial feeling when they watched the CCTV back in the tapas restaurant.

'It would have been one year next week,' Jennifer had said, the shock of the past tense she was using settling on her like a piercing, cold rain. 'But I wasn't going to see Alex next week because he had planned to be in Suffolk with Amelia, so I gave him the bracelet last night.'

Hana nodded, unable to say that she was sorry, although she felt it. Affairs were tricky things and although she had no judgement about it — how could she possibly understand the nuance and truth of a relationship from being part of a conversation that had lasted only minutes — but having just left the grieving wife, she felt like she had to be neutral for both parties.

'You said when we arrived that you knew it had been Alexander who was shot at the station last night. Why did you think that?' asked Hana.

'I just had a feeling. A terrible, terrible feeling. It was all over the news and I couldn't call or text him.'

'Why not?'

'We have a rule about it. Or at least Alex does. Obviously, I wouldn't care at all. But when we are not together, he is the one who calls or texts. If I don't respond to a text within five minutes, I simply don't. He said it was too risky in case his wife ever saw anything. So last night I didn't text him when I heard what had happened. But I know Alex...'

Jennifer's emotion suddenly caught up with her and she struggled to get the words out, the tears now coming hard and fast. Sharma stood up again to find her some tissues.

'I just knew...' Jennifer stuttered. 'I knew that he would have called me right away to tell me he was safe when the shooting happened. He was so thoughtful. He knew I would have been worried. But then he didn't call. I just knew.'

Sharma handed Jennifer a crumpled ball of tissues, which she accepted.

Hana suddenly felt exhausted. She had spent the past few hours with two women, both grieving the same unlucky man. Unless this wasn't about luck at all but why weren't they seeing it?

Thirty

There was someone unexpected at the station when Luke and Fiona returned.

'She just showed up here?' Luke asked Rowdy.

'Yes, I've put her into Interview Room One. She seems a bit frantic.'

'Okay, thanks. Please have someone get her a cup of tea.'

'Already done. I don't think she's touched it though.'

Luke nodded and excused himself, figuring that Fiona Holland would have no difficulty introducing herself to Laura Rowdy and making herself at home. Hana, Sharma and Lombardi weren't back yet and Henry also seemed to be taking his sweet time getting to Scotland Yard.

Luke looked towards the espresso machine and then decided against it. He felt jittery enough as it was.

He walked down the hall and knocked softly on the door of the Interview Room and then stepped inside.

'Mrs. Alpine, hello. I'm sorry that you've been stuck in here. It's not the most comfortable room but it was designed that way. We usually have criminals in here,' Luke said.

Trevor Alpine's mother wasn't soothed by this little joke.

'What can I do for you?' Luke asked.

'There's something I didn't say earlier today. I've had an argument with my husband about it and that's why he's not here. But it's my son. I need to know what happened to him.'

Luke thought — we do know what happened to him. He was on a date and was shot through the neck. What Trevor Alpine's mother was desperate to know was *why* this had happened to her son.

'Go ahead.'

Mrs. Alpine took a deep breath and turned the paper cup of tea around in her hands.

'My son very specifically told me that if I ever didn't hear from him for more than two weeks, that I was to be in touch with Morgan Lewis. You met him this morning at my son's flat.'

'Go on.'

'That's it,' said Mrs. Alpine. 'That's why Morgan Lewis was there. I know you were wondering why I had called him. But when I questioned Morgan about why my son said I should be in touch with him if he ever was away for more than two weeks, Morgan said he didn't know. I think he's lying.'

'Do you think Morgan Lewis has something to do with why your son was shot?'

'Very possibly.'

As she said this, Mrs. Alpine's voice seemed to give out on her and she barely got the words out.

Luke reached across the table and gently touched her arm.

'We'll speak to Morgan Lewis, Mrs. Alpine. We'll get to the bottom of this so you can have some answers.'

'Thank you.'

'But one more thing before you leave,' said Luke. 'Did your son often disappear for large chunks of time — two weeks as you say? Or more?'

'Yes,' Mrs. Alpine replied. 'But never for more than two weeks and he always called the second he got back.'

'Where did he go?'

'He always just said Eastern Europe. I figured it was a work trip and he was jumping around all of those small countries over there since he was gone for such a stretch.'

'Okay, thanks for coming in.'

Luke escorted Mrs. Alpine back to reception and was on the phone to Hana before he even set foot back in his office.

'Where are you?' Luke said.

'I'm with Lombardi and Sharma and we're on our way back now. Alexander Mathison was having an affair. We just met the lover. She is distraught.'

Luke closed his eyes in frustration. There were too many leads, too many paths to go down, and this inevitably meant that they were going to waste time going down the wrong one.

'She gave him the bracelet,' Luke said.

'Exactly.'

Hana sounded upbeat and confident, like she was about to figure the whole thing out. Luke figured he may as well go with her mood and filled her in on Mrs. Alpine's visit.

'So I need you to pay a quick visit to Morgan Lewis,' Luke said. 'He knows something and we need that information.'

'Did the toxicology report come back on Trevor Alpine?'

Luke closed his eyes again.

'I'll check. But please come straight back here when you've finished with Morgan Lewis. I think all hell is about to break loose.'

'Meaning?'

'You'll see when you get here.'

The toxicology report proved Hana right. Trevor Alpine had traces of cocaine in his system. They were trace amounts, which meant that he had not taken any cocaine the night that he was killed, but he had in the day or so before that.

This would be nice for Lisa Owens to know — that her date wasn't high when they were last together — but beyond that, all this information did was create a bigger web of confusion for the detectives to try to crawl through.

When Luke called Hana to tell her all of this, he let her know that Lisa Owens had been discharged from the hospital. Hana seemed a bit elated by all of this news — the fact that someone had escaped the intention of the shooter and was alive and out of the hospital, and that her hunch that Trevor Alpine was a cocaine user was correct.

'That's great, Luke. Thanks. We'll report back to the Incident Room as soon as we've finished with Morgan Lewis.'

Hana was at the wheel, speeding aggressively through London to the address they'd been given for Morgan Lewis. At a traffic light she picked up her phone and opened it with her face recognition, before handing it to Sharma.

'I'm going to need you to work your magic even from the car,' she said. 'Open my Photo Library and one of the last photos is of a series of Euro coins. I need to know what country they're from.'

'Okay,' said Sharma from the backseat.

'And no scrolling any further back. I don't know you well enough for you to see my nude pics.'

The look on Sharma's face was absolutely priceless. Hana was staring at him reflected in the rear view mirror and burst out laughing. Lombardi didn't know what to think. She was relieved that Hana was joking, but also wouldn't put it past her to have this kind of photo somewhere on her camera roll.

This really wasn't the day that either Sharma or Lombardi had expected.

THIRTY-ONE

'How seriously do we take this threat?'

Luke looked at Fiona Holland as did the others in the room.

'You're MI5. You tell me.' Luke replied.

Luke had nothing against Fiona Holland. She was just doing her job and if she felt she needed to be there, then so be it. Who was he to question MI5? But he didn't like her being in the Incident Room. It was his room and it didn't feel right.

Henry MacAskill was also there and the conversation was slightly muted as he didn't have the security clearance for anyone to speak freely, but there were decisions that had to be made and he was inevitably going to be a part of that.

The email that had come into Henry had been analyzed by the tech analysts as Sharma was still out in the field with Lombardi and Hana. They had immediately said that it wouldn't be quick to track down the IP address or any other detail of who had sent it.

'Why not?' O'Donnell had barked at them.

'Because, Sir, the email was sent using a VPN as well as an anonymous and encrypted email server. And there's no attachment to the email, so there is no metadata to scrape. We'll eventually be able to get something for you, but it will take a bit of time.'

For once, Luke was relieved that it wasn't Sharma breaking this kind of news to O'Donnell. He was well out of it and much safer from the wrath of the Super while he was out interviewing Morgan Lewis.

The problem was that the one thing they really didn't have was time.

Luke looked over at the email that Henry had received, the image transposed onto the board at the front of the room. They certainly felt that it was genuine. Even though unusual crimes, especially murders, tended to bring out the average crazy person who sent mail to the media, or the police, this one knew about the previous note.

DON'T DELAY. PRINT THE WARNING.
I'LL BE WATCHING.
TUUM EST

Next to the image of the email was Fiona's handwritten translation of the latin words.

It's up to you.

The sinister nature of the email had everyone even more on edge.

'Look, the Editor-in-Chief is willing to print the content of the note,' Henry said.

'Oh I'm sure she is,' Fiona shot back. 'So the rest of the media can run with the story, and more people buy your paper tomorrow than ever before. The freshly lined pockets of your shareholders will be thrilled.'

'I'm not sure that it's entirely financially motivated,' Henry argued back. 'This is a major piece of news and the public has the right to know what is happening.'

'Not if it further endangers the public.'

Luke sighed and realized that the sigh was very much

audible as the room looked over at him. They weren't getting anywhere.

'Your thoughts please, DCI Wiley?' Fiona said.

'I don't see any point in printing the warning until we have figured out — or ruled out — any connections between the three shootings. Do we have an ID on the Hyde Park victim yet?'

Rowdy shook her head.

'Fine, well, we should regroup when Hana, Lombardi and Sharma return.'

The door to the Incident Room flung open and a very excited, very wet dog bounded inside.

'Sorry, Sir,' said Officer Parker, running to catch up with it.

'We've been to the lab and samples have been taken, so I took her down to the garage and gave her a good bath where the cars are washed.'

Luke couldn't help but smile.

'Well done, Parker. What are you going to call him for the time being?'

'I thought Steve might be a good fit. Doesn't he look like a Steve?'

Luke couldn't believe that the kid had such a good sense of humour. Stephen O'Donnell, however, was not at all amused and turned to head back to his office, barking that someone should let him know when everyone else was back.

'I'm not sure that Ms. Holland enjoys the company of canines,' Luke said.

'Oh, really? I'm sorry, Ma'am. I'll take him out.'

'Steve will be chipped if we're lucky. We can ID the victim from that if we're really lucky. Dr. Chung will likely have a scanner and Rowdy can run the data for you.'

'Yes, Sir.'

Parker picked up the wire terrier and stroked the top of his head.

'Come on, Steve, let's figure out exactly who you are.'

———

Henry had been excused and he headed back to the paper to await any last minute change of heart by the detectives. For now, the message would not run.

Rowdy, Luke and Fiona were staring at the board when the others finally returned. Lombardi and Sharma seemed exhilarated to have been out of the Incident Room for much of the day.

'Fiona, this is Joy Lombardi and Bobby Sharma. They are completely indispensable and I now don't function without them,' said Luke.

Fiona shook both of their hands. When she didn't volunteer exactly where she had arrived from, Luke took the liberty of telling them.

'We have MI5 with us for the time being, it seems.'

'Oh, right,' said Sharma.

Hana appeared at the door to the Incident Room and stopped short when she saw that there was someone new in the room.

'Hi,' Luke said. 'You're back. We can get started.'

'Hello, Hana,' Fiona said.

Luke was the one who now stopped short as he was walking towards the board. He turned to stare at Hana. And then at Fiona.

How did they know each other?

Rowdy raised her eyebrows at Luke. This was clearly news to her as well.

Hana did not respond to Fiona, but looked past her at Luke.

'You could have told me that MI5 had been called in.'

Luke did not want to apologize to Hana in front of everyone else. He would do so later, right after he asked her what the hell was going on and how she was acquainted with this very senior officer from the Secret Services.

'Can you fill us in on your various visits today? Do they bring us closer to a connection between the shootings?' Luke asked Hana.

'I'm not seeing it. But let's start with Trevor Alpine. After the visit from his mother today, we finally tracked down Morgan Lewis. He wasn't at home, but we found him at his gym. I think a second visit by three officers freaked him out and that cockiness from this morning had vanished. Thanks to Sharma here, we knew that the coins I found in his desk drawer were from Lithuania and when I questioned him about that country, it all came out.'

'And?'

'Dodgy property deals that he and Trevor Alpine were doing the legal paperwork for. Lithuanian investors. That's where Trevor was disappearing to, and Morgan said that these guys often took away mobile phones and other ways to communicate. He was clearly a bit spooked and that's why he told his mother to contact Morgan if he was ever longer than two weeks.'

'So did Morgan take anything from Trevor's flat this morning, as the officer suspected?'

'He sure did,' Sharma said, pulling a document out from his jacket and holding it in the air.

'Some legal papers pertaining to the current case,' Lombardi continued.

'And there was a bit of coke snorted from time to time with the clients,' Hana said. 'The fact that we knew that freaked him out even more.'

'Do you think he is involved in Trevor's death?' Luke asked.

'Highly doubt it,' said Hana. 'Could be a Lithuanian mobster, but I don't know why they'd murder the person who is facilitating their deals. Doesn't make sense.'

'Do we see any connection at all between Trevor Alpine and Alexander Mathison apart from the fact that they are both lawyers?' Luke asked the room.

It was Sharma who offered his opinion first.

'I don't see it, Sir. I've gone through both of their client lists extensively and there is no overlap. They don't even practice the same type of law. There are a lot of lawyers in London. It's likely a coincidence.'

'And the affair that was ongoing between Alexander Mathison and Jennifer Clunes,' Luke said. 'Are we certain that Jennifer was otherwise unattached? And that Amelia Mathison was not also playing around?'

'Nothing that we can find,' said Lombardi. 'I don't think we have a jealous lover wanting to shoot Alexander Mathison so he's out of the way.'

'And we can't yet ID the man who was executed in Hyde Park,' Luke said. 'Well, I think we're all doing a smashing job with this, don't you?'

The room was silent.

THIRTY-TWO

Hana had offered to give Luke a lift home, even though it was the opposite direction for her. She knew that while she didn't exactly owe Luke an explanation, she did have to tell him about Fiona.

'It has been an absolute clusterfuck of a day, Hana.'

'I know.'

Hana appreciated that Luke hadn't immediately jumped at her with questions when they got into the car and finally had a moment alone. It had started to rain and it had already been dark for a few hours, which made the evening seem longer and colder than it actually was. Rain in December tended to do that.

'So are you going to tell me how you know an MI5 agent?'

'Oh I thought we were just going to ignore that.'

'Nice try, Hana.'

'I obviously didn't know she was going to be in the room when I got back there today.'

'I think the look on your face when you walked in made that pretty clear.'

'She wasn't MI5 when I knew her.'

'Is this going to be quite the story?' Luke asked.

'Depends on what you consider quite the story.'

'I'm not heading out anywhere tonight,' Luke said. 'I've got some time.'

Hana and Luke both flinched slightly at Luke's first sentiment. The thought of going out to a restaurant or a bar, or to go for a walk, or to be in any tube or train station, wasn't exactly appealing. They shouldn't have felt nervous about doing so, especially as the rest of the public were out enjoying all that London had to offer, but they did.

'I'm shattered,' Hana said. 'So rain check?'

'Sure, I'm actually seeing Nicky at 6am tomorrow morning.'

'On a Sunday?'

'Yeah. I do take note of the texts you send me. Yours was pretty clear about me getting off my ass and telling Nicky about the photographs. So I'm going to tell her tomorrow.'

Hana felt enormously relieved to hear this. She needed Luke to have a clear head, especially when cases like the one they were working on now came along. He needed more support than she was able to give him.

'Do you have any idea of what exactly you're going to say to her?'

'Not really. I think I'm just going to tell her exactly what has happened. I mean, I'm not going to go into the individual cases that we've gone back to or discuss exactly who the killer could be. I just need her to know what has happened to me. To us.'

'Thank you.'

'I honestly don't know how I'm going to get through it,' Luke said. 'I'm dreading it.'

'Oh that's easy,' said Hana. 'Just think about how much you love your wife.'

They continued driving on towards Islington and Hana

felt she should reciprocate Luke's gesture, so she told him about Fiona. About how they had met when they were both in the military.

'It was a long time ago,' Hana said. 'Fiona was my commanding officer. And she was a damn good one, too. I knew she had been recruited to MI5 — an old colleague had told me that — but I'm not surprised at how quickly she has risen up those ranks.'

'Some people are just good at getting promoted,' Luke said, thinking of O'Donnell.

'You don't know the half of it,' Hana murmured.

'What?'

'Nothing. It's not important. I was just taken aback to see her there in the Incident Room. It had been a long time.'

What she wasn't saying was that Fiona Holland had been directly responsible for Hana leaving the armed forces. Hana had made a mistake. A massive error of judgement. She had trusted someone she shouldn't have.

'You just looked like you didn't want her there. It seemed like a bit more than surprise to me,' Luke said.

Hana sighed.

'It rather was. I was sleeping with her.'

Thirty-Three

Nicky Bowman had never before offered a Sunday appointment, let alone a 6am appointment.

She had set her alarm for 5am although she woke before it, and set about turning up the thermostat in the house so that it was warm when Luke arrived. She had a quick cup of coffee to wake herself up and considered jumping in the shower to freshen up and really ensure that she was alert, but decided against it. There was something that felt good about acknowledging that this was an exception, that she was allowing the importance of whatever Luke needed to see her about. Getting in the shower and washing her hair and looking as she usually would for a weekday session seemed inappropriate somehow. So Nicky threw on a pair of worn, comfy jeans that were usually reserved for her down time on the weekend, and a favourite jumper, and got the proper pot of coffee assembled and ready to brew in time for Luke's arrival.

Luke had also woken before his alarm. This didn't surprise him.

His mind was too full of the three shootings and the tremendous anxiety about what was going to happen next. He couldn't be sure that they had made the right call to not print the warning from the killer. He also couldn't believe that they didn't seem any closer to catching the bastard than they had the moment he abruptly returned from his holiday.

But even if the case had been closed and he wasn't hunting a sadistic killer, he would have tossed and turned all night in anticipation of this session with his therapist. This was the session he had been putting off for months and finally it was upon him.

He tried to focus on what Hana had said to him in the car when she dropped him off at home just hours earlier.

Think about how much you love your wife.

It was going to be a long day, so Luke took a long, hot shower, letting the water feel like it was piercing his skin. Feeling at least a little bit more invigorated when he stepped out of the shower, he found a pair of grey trousers that had only come back from the dry cleaner earlier that week and put them on. Wearing all freshly laundered clothes, he finished towelling his hair as dry as he could and headed downstairs to have a coffee before driving to Nicky's house. He certainly wasn't going to walk over at this time of the morning and there was also a tiny itch in the back of his brain that he was desperate not to scratch. It was an itch that said: Be careful. There's a killer out there.

The anxiety amongst his colleagues was affecting him. He didn't want to believe that it was the actions of the killer that had gotten to him, but perhaps a little bit had seeped into what he was feeling. Luke constantly felt like he was looking over his shoulder.

When he got to Nicky's house, he looked at it from the street. He had been here in the dark before, when it was winter and the light of the day faded early. But the rest of the street had been awake with lights on in the other houses and people walking dogs or on their way home. This morning, this street in north London was still asleep apart from the lights on in Nicky's house, the faint yellow beaming out onto the walkway that led to the house from the pavement. It was like a light that was inviting him in, inviting him to reveal the one thing he hadn't been able to tell her.

Luke hesitated before ringing the doorbell, worried that the sound would seem overly harsh in the silent morning, so he rapped softly on the front door with his knuckles.

Nicky had been waiting downstairs for him and opened the door with a smile and a nod, just as she always did.

'Good morning,' she said.

'Hi.'

'Go on upstairs, I'll bring up the coffee.'

Luke could smell the coffee and the scent was almost intoxicating at this time of the morning. He felt immediately more at ease seeing Nicky's warm, open face. The comfort that this fifty minutes of his day, the comfort of this woman and her house gave him was such a gift. He felt ready to say what he needed to say.

As he climbed the stairs to Nicky's office, he noticed that the house felt a bit different at 6am. It was probably because Luke was entering his therapist's private time, a space that felt more personal. He knew he would think about the next hour for the rest of the day and carry it with him as a sort of talisman in what was going to be an extremely difficult shift at Scotland Yard.

'Thank you for seeing me so early in the morning. And on a Sunday. I really appreciate it,' Luke said as Nicky handed him a steaming cup of black coffee.

She poured a bit of milk into her own cup and nodded, but didn't say anything. She was waiting for him to begin.

And then he had difficulty beginning.

'I knew that work was going to make it tough to meet this

week,' Luke said. 'Obviously these shootings are taking up a lot of time.'

'I saw you on the news yesterday. It looks quite serious.'

'It is.'

Luke paused, unsure of how to continue, how to get these words about his wife's death out of his mouth.

'You don't talk about the details of your work very often here. Is that what is concerning you?'

Luke sipped his coffee, which was still extremely hot, but his throat suddenly felt very dry and he tried to relieve it.

'No,' he said.

Nicky sat very still in her chair, her legs tucked up underneath her, a concession to the unusual hour and circumstances of their meeting.

'There is something that I haven't told you and it's gotten to the point where I need to. I'm struggling with it, I mean, obviously I'm struggling with it. It's 6am on a Sunday morning and I'm sitting here. Hana has been insisting I tell you.'

'Hana knows the thing that you haven't been able to share with me?'

'Yes.'

'That's good,' Nicky said.

Luke hadn't thought about it this way — that Hana knowing what he knew was a good thing. He had felt that it was Hana's burden as well, a burden that they shared. But maybe by sharing it, they could manage it a little bit easier.

'When I went back to work when Chloe Little was murdered and was dragged back into the old Marcus Wright case, something happened.'

Nicky was sitting very still.

'I came home from work and an envelope had been shoved through my letterbox. The envelope contained photographs of Sadie.'

Luke took a deep breath for what he was about to say next.

'In the photographs, Sadie was sitting in her car in the moments just before her death. Just before the car veered off the road into the lake. And there is someone else in the car with her. This person forced the car off the road. This person caused Sadie's death.'

Luke looked at Nicky to try to gauge her reaction, the relief that the words had been able to get out of his mouth already beginning to flood his body. She did not say anything, so Luke continued.

'One of the photographs is of the car submerged in the lake. The photographer, the person who killed Sadie, took it from right next to the car. She was in there drowning while he took it.'

At this description of the final photograph Luke had pulled out of the envelope on that terrible day, the photograph that he now looked at the most, Nicky's hand flew up to her mouth and covered it. It was an involuntary reaction and she gasped.

'Oh my god, Luke.'

'Yes,' he said quietly. 'I know.'

'When was this again?'

'About three months ago.'

'You haven't said anything here in all that time.'

Nicky said this as a statement, not a question, as if she was trying to confirm this for herself and what that meant.

'What have the police said?' Nicky asked.

Luke shook his head very slowly, from side to side.

'You haven't told them?'

'No. It's extremely important that they do not know for now.'

'Why on earth not?'

Luke put down his coffee and leaned forward. He needed

Nicky to clearly hear and understand what he was about to say next.

'Nicky, this is one of the reasons I haven't told you before now. I am going to ask you not to say anything. To anyone. I know that this puts you in a bit of a murky spot. Ethically, you need to report a crime. I'm asking you to see that technically in the eyes of the law at this point in time, no crime has been committed. I need time to work this out. Hana and I are trying to figure out what happened.'

Nicky wiped her top lip, as if she had noticed that she was sweating. It was clear that Luke had spent a great deal of time thinking through this scenario — of what would happen when he told her. And ethically? If any of her patients had come to her with even a hypothetical situation like the one Luke just described, and asked her if she would have to now break patient/therapist confidentiality, she wouldn't have a fucking clue.

'Okay,' she said. 'I can do that.'

Luke looked enormously relieved.

'Thank you.'

'But Luke, this is extremely serious.'

Luke couldn't help but smile at her.

'You've said that to me before.'

'I mean it, Luke. Do you and Hana have any idea of who has done this? Who is involved?'

Luke took a sip of coffee and thought that he didn't know much about anything right now. He didn't know who had killed his wife and he didn't know who had killed three people in the centre of London over the past three days.

'That's the thing,' Luke said. 'Hana and I are going crazy trying to work it out. The envelope was not posted, it was hand delivered, so that feels like it's someone who knows me. It may be someone from the Met.'

'You suspect police involvement?'

'I do. Hana is unsure. But I've gone through every single case of mine over the past five years looking for anyone who may have had a grudge with me, or didn't like wealthy people like my wife, or had some sort of vendetta. No one is obvious. I can't seem to see it and...'

Luke trailed off, unable to describe in the way he wished, how much not knowing who had killed his wife was affecting him. But he also knew that he didn't need to tell Nicky that. She would know.

They continued to talk for the rest of the fifty minute session, Nicky wanting to ensure that Luke was taking care of himself during all of this. They discussed the small rituals he had put in place with Nicky's help after Sadie died. The moments of the day he set aside to speak to her. The choice to walk somewhere instead of driving, and to walk without listening to music, but only to his own thoughts.

Luke found himself trying to reassure his therapist that he was going to be alright. He had absolutely no idea if this was true or not.

'And maybe look at things a different way. Sometimes we become completely blinkered by what we think we know and we end up looking in the wrong place.'

'What do you mean?' Luke asked.

'I don't mean anything in particular. But if you say that you've looked at every single case and every single person who could have a problem with you or with your wife, maybe that's the wrong place to look. Maybe that's not the connection.'

'Maybe.'

'I'm going to say something that I really don't want you to take the wrong way.'

Oh god, Luke thought. This can't be good. He didn't say anything, waiting for Nicky to finish her thought and hoping that his silence would give her permission to say whatever she wanted to say. He was too anxious to verbally tell her to go ahead.

'How well do you think you know your wife?' Nicky said.

The question threw Luke entirely. His immediate reaction was one of anger. He wanted to shout at Nicky. How dare you question how well I know my wife — of course I know my wife.

But he didn't shout and he didn't react. He was curious enough, and desperate enough, to let his therapist continue.

'There just may be something about her that you didn't know. Look, I'm not the detective, but if I was, that's probably where I'd start.'

Luke stood up to leave and realized that he had been with Nicky for well over an hour.

'I'm sorry, I didn't see the time. I'll pay for two sessions.'

Nicky waved her hand, as if she was batting away the offer.

'Don't worry about it.'

'Thanks.'

Luke stopped when he got to the door and turned back to look at Nicky.

'What do you have planned for your day?'

The question took her aback, partly because she wondered if he wanted to keep talking, and partly because she didn't know what the rest of her day looked like.

'I haven't really thought about it yet.'

'Nicky, if you don't have to go out today, that would be best.'

They looked at each other, Nicky suddenly feeling something that she hadn't felt for about nine years, not since her husband died.

Fear.

THIRTY-FOUR

They had not done as they were told.
There would be consequences.
Tuum est. It's up to you.
There was a part of him that knew this was going to happen, that they would not listen. He had prepared the next instruction.

Trafalgar Square was bustling with people on a Sunday before Christmas, just approaching lunchtime. It was a good day to be in the square because unlike weekdays, where you would see mostly tourists — a few workers nearby on the Strand or Pall Mall dashing through on their way to somewhere else perhaps — this wasn't the case on a Sunday.

On a Sunday you had lots of Londoners in the National Gallery. They viewed the glorious works of arts and then streamed out of the front door and down the large stone steps into the centre of the square.

He had been taken to the National Gallery once. He remembers being told to stand in front of the "masterpieces" and be very still. He preferred the lush colours of the more modern paintings, the ones where you could still see the globs of paint on the canvas, like the paintings were somehow alive.

He could not have been more than seven years old and he remembers the maze of hallways and large rooms. The doors that led to more doors that led to other staircases and he felt like he was in a puzzle that he couldn't escape from. He remembers needing to get out and that he couldn't. He remembers that he was late. He was very late and there would be consequences.

There would be consequences again today.

The man stood to the side of the gallery, watching the crowds. Families were gathered watching a street performer, his batons of fire flying high into the air. Shoppers were milling around, giant bags banging against their legs. A couple of teenagers were skateboarding.

Who was he going to choose?

He stood in the square for almost an hour observing everyone around him. He was choosing not to rush.

He spied a young man in a brown leather jacket. The jacket looked worn and comfortable and he was constantly pulling out a mobile phone from its pocket and checking it. The young man was waiting for someone. The young man was being impatient. That wouldn't do.

As the young man began to move across the square towards Canada House, he did the same, following closely behind him. He took the note out of his own pocket and reached forward to slip it into the jacket pocket of the young man in front of him.

Wasn't this fun, he thought. Placing the note on the body before I've even killed him.

The young man was engrossed in his phone, continuing to be impatient, and did not notice the sleight of hand that had just occurred.

'Pardon me,' he said, tapping the young man on the shoulder.

The young man whipped around to see who had touched him and he imagined that the young man's face was one of surprise as he shot him in the chest.

This time he helped the man to the ground, as he went limp and careened forward into him. This time the shot was definitely heard and the crowd scattered much more quickly than it had done in the station.

This time the man knew he was going to be on camera, and he didn't care.

Thirty-Five

Hana was already in the office when Luke had arrived that morning.

'Good morning,' he said. 'I wasn't expecting to see you in so early today.'

'In all honesty, I just wanted to get some work done before Fiona gets here.'

'Ah, right.'

Hana leaned back in her chair and stretched.

'Something did occur to me though as I was driving in this morning. We've actually missed something.'

'What's that?' Luke said, fiddling with the espresso machine which seemed to have a coffee pod still stuck in it from the day before.

'We keep going round and round in circles trying to find a connection between these people who have been shot. Yesterday we came to the conclusion that there was no connection. And that's pretty shit considering that we have three murders and one attempted murder on our hands. If it's some psychopath picking off random people, we are stuffed.'

'I'm sorry is this your morning pep talk?' Luke said. 'I'm loving it. It's really setting me up for the day.'

Hana rolled her eyes and continued.

'We do have a connection. It's been right in front of us the whole time. The connection is Henry MacAskill.'

Luke squinted and inserted a new coffee pod into the machine.

'I know that Henry is a prominent journalist, and a good one, but why are the notes and the email being addressed specifically to him? Why not to the paper in general, or to a different journalist?'

'You have an answer already, don't you?'

Hana ignored him.

'I went back and looked at the last year of Henry's articles in the paper. Lots of reporting on various news stories, of course, but he also wrote a series of articles about the trauma he suffered at boarding school. There are seven pieces altogether and the comment section under each one shows a hell of a lot of people who felt the same.'

'People who hated their school? That's not exactly uncommon.'

'No, it's not,' said Hana. 'But if our shooter has this particular grievance, then it makes sense that he's sending letters to Henry.'

'You think the Latin in the notes is from his school?'

'Or he learnt Latin in school.'

Luke sipped his coffee and thought about it. It made a lot of sense, but it still wasn't going to help them find this psychopath.

———

The team had been a bit jumpy all morning so when the call came in just after eleven o'clock that there had been a disturbance in Trafalgar Square, they leapt up as if the gunshot had actually ricocheted through the Incident Room.

'Shit,' Luke said. 'He went through with it.'

O'Donnell looked utterly panicked. Luke could almost see the wheels turning in his head that were concerned solely with his own reputation. Yet another shooting in central London. A bad call about not printing the killer's message. He knew that Marina Scott-Carson would be down to the seventh floor at any moment.

Luke and Hana didn't have time for second guessing the decision that was made yesterday.

'Trafalgar Square must be one of the most covered locations in London. Get those cameras up, Sharma. I want to see all of them.'

Fiona Holland had arrived and was standing in the doorway.

'That's some timing,' Hana said to her, as she waited for the CCTV to be pulled up.

'Somebody has to go to the scene. I can go and take one of my officers wth me.'

Hana nodded at her.

It was all taking too long.

'Come on, Sharma.'

Luke was almost shouting now, checking his watch as well as the clock that hung on the wall.

'Coming, coming,' Sharma said, typing with a speed that actually blurred his fingers.

'Got it. It's up. There are six main cameras. They should all be there.'

The team swivelled to face the monitor next to the board and six windows appeared. The time stamp said 10:55am.

It took them a moment to spot the shooter but when he fired the gun into the chest of the man in the brown leather jacket, the entire crowd were like a handful of beads that were dropped from a height, scattering everywhere as they hit the floor.

'Let's work the footage backwards from here please,' Hana said.

'The son of a bitch,' Luke said. 'There he is. In plain sight.'

The man was not disguised in any way. He wasn't wearing a hoodie, he wasn't wearing any kind of hat or face mask. He was in khaki trousers and black boots. On his top was a grey overcoat. He was, as they already knew, of average height and build. Now they could see that he had short, light brown hair and a slight cleft in his chin. He was absolutely unremarkable.

Except that he was a cold blooded killer.

'He's not even bothering to hide or to run. Look at him. He knows that he's on camera. He knows that we have him,' Hana said.

'That's what worries me,' said Luke. 'This is a guy with nothing to lose.'

THIRTY-SIX

harma had the facial recognition running within ten minutes and when he suddenly exclaimed, Luke and Hana and Lombardi immediately stopped what they were doing.

'Holy shit,' Sharma said.

'I've never heard you swear before,' Lombardi said with surprise.

'Well holy shit, look at this,' Sharma replied, pointing to the monitor.

It was a still image of the shooter, easily captured by the Trafalgar Square cameras, next to another image of the same man.

'Where is this?' said Luke.

'You're not going to believe this, but it's the Dog and Duck. It's taken just minutes after the shooting in the train station. He didn't go out the back door by the bathrooms and to the side street. He must have dumped his tweed coat and his hoodie out there in the rubbish bins and then come back inside. I'll bet you ten quid that we're going to find his clothing in there when the search is done.'

The shooter was wearing a blazer in the pub footage, which he must have been wearing over the hoodie, but under the coat.

'That's why we didn't spot it.'

'Is he ordering a fucking drink?' Hana asked.

'It would appear so, Ma'am,' said Sharma.

Hana and Luke looked at each other. They were thinking the same thing so there was no need to say it aloud.

This guy was dangerous. Anyone this cavalier with their identity after three shootings was a big, big problem.

'Where is Fiona? Is she at the scene yet?'

Rowdy was on the phone and she held her hand up as if to tell them to hold on. She was nodding. Then she pointed to the screen at the front of the room.

'What?' Luke mouthed.

Rowdy hung up and turned her attention to the screen.

'You're going to want to see this.'

Flashing up on the screen, sent into Rowdy from Fiona who had reached the victim in Trafalgar Square, was another note. This one was also handwritten in block letters and black ink.

PUBLISH ON THE WEBSITE TODAY OR MORE WILL DIE

TARDE VENIENTIBUS OSSA
VIRTUS IMPAVIDA

'Where the hell did this one come from?' Hana asked.

'From the victim's jacket pocket,' said Rowdy. 'Fiona is with the body now.'

Sharma squinted at the footage on the monitor and backed it up again. They had to look closely. It happened so quickly and so effortlessly that they had missed it the first time. The shooter's hand slipping into the man's jacket pocket, depositing his warning, a deadly sleight of hand.

'What does it mean? Anyone?' Luke said.

'I've got it,' said Lombardi, as she jumped up and began to write next to the Latin phrases on the board.

To the late are left the bones.

Fearless virtue.

'What the hell does that all mean?' said Hana.

Luke looked up at Laura Rowdy, hoping to find some sort of solace, but there was none.

'Rowdy, we need Henry and Marina here. We have a big decision to make.'

————

The decision needed to be made quickly and in the end, Henry MacAskill and Marina Scott-Carson agreed on the approach and gave their respective sign offs.

The two Latin phrases would be printed on the paper's website within the next fifteen minutes, which would hopefully circumvent any further executions in the centre of London today.

The city had emptied out, seemingly instantly.

The team watched the rolling news broadcast from the Incident Room. Major streets like Piccadilly and Regent Street were deserted. Many shops had made the decision to shut for the remainder of the day. The tube and buses were still running, but there were very few people on them.

News had leaked that the death in Hyde Park the previous day had also been a shooting.

People were terrified to step outside. They were right to be frightened.

There was no pattern to the shootings, all seemingly random, and anyone could be next.

The two Latin phrases would feature on the landing page of the paper's website, with the accompanying copy asking the public if the two phrases, when associated together like this, struck a chord or had a particular meaning to them. The police were asking for the public's assistance and a contact form was provided when you clicked through the link on the website article.

'God knows if this is going to work,' Hana said. 'How many people do we have waiting to go through the forms? I can't even imagine how many we're going to get.'

'Sharma, does anything pop up for you with these phrases?' Luke asked.

Sharma could only shake his head, his eyes not moving from his computer screen, as he desperately looked for a link.

It didn't take long at all.

Luke could have thanked the entire population of people who lived almost entirely online, a group for which he usually felt enormous disdain.

A young analyst who had been sent upstairs to the seventh floor to help field contact forms ran into the Incident Room, still holding her laptop in her hands.

'Sir, I think this one might be something.'

Luke and Hana rushed over and read what was on the screen. And then Luke picked up his mobile and made the call.

THIRTY-SEVEN

The retired headmaster had recognized the Latin phrases right away.

'It's the combination of them that made them jump out at me,' he said. 'Fearless Virtue is the school motto.'

The school was, as Hana had aptly predicted, a boarding school in Yorkshire. The headmaster had worked there for many years and was shocked to see two Latin phrases that he knew very well appearing with an appeal on the front page of the Times.

'What is the second phrase? To the late are left the bones. It seems unusual,' said Luke.

'Yes, exactly. It is unusual. Not a common turn of phrase at all. But it was the favourite phrase of a teacher who used to work here. He used to say it all the time, and in a rather demeaning way. I never particularly cared for it. Or for him. The meaning behind the phrase is really that if you are late, or tardy, or a bit lost in your way, life will give you nothing.'

'What was this teacher's name?'

'Conrad Clifton. He just recently died.'

'How recently?'

'About a month.'

There is was, Luke thought and he could see that Hana was now in a standing position, listening to this conversation. They almost had him.

'Did Conrad Clifton have a son?' asked Luke.

'He did. Bart Clifton. And he had a daughter as well. I believe her name was Eleanor.'

Luke didn't have to do anything else except thank the headmaster for taking the time to send in the form. Hana was already out the door with Rowdy, finding an address for Bart Clifton.

———

Within ten minutes, Luke and Hana were sitting in the back of a tactical response team van, racing up to Hyde Park Corner and then further west.

'The son of a bitch lives right by the third shooting,' Hana said.

Luke had never seen the roads so quiet. The public was staying inside, away from the crosshairs of a gun and away from the randomness of a potential tragedy.

It probably wasn't going to be you that is shot, but what if it was?

The van sirens screamed as they sped down Knightbridge and past Harrods, down Brompton Road to the Victoria and Albert Museum and the Science Museum and then turning right so sharply towards the park that Luke and Hana had to grab onto anything they could in order to not crash into each other. Their guns were ready to go.

The second tactical team that had approached from the north side had reached the building first and the detectives could see a line of burly men in black armoured uniforms streaming out of the vehicle and surrounding the flat on all sides.

Their van came to a screeching stop and Hana and Luke jumped out, their own bullet proof vests feeling surprisingly light as they ran the last half block towards the flat. This was adrenaline, Hana thought, knowing that the vest weighed almost a quarter of her own body weight.

'Hold back please,' said the Commander, his arm outstretched to stop Hana and Luke from proceeding any further.

'Is he in there?' Hana said.

'One moment, Ma'am. They'll have it cleared in just a moment.'

The Commander's radio squawked and he pressed the button on its side.

'Go ahead.'

'Clear, Sir. The flat is empty.'

Luke and Hana could not have looked more defeated, and more angry, if they tried.

'Fuck,' Luke swore under his breath.

'We're going in,' Hana said to the Commander.

'Yes, Ma'am,' he replied, stepping aside to let Luke and Hana past him and down the half dozen stairs to the basement flat.

They walked in the front door which had been broken open by the tactical team, its wooden frame splintered into several pieces.

'Is there anything useful here?' Luke asked an officer who was standing just inside the door.

'Just this fellow,' he replied.

Luke looked down at an old springer spaniel, excitedly wagging his tail. He bent down to look at the dog's collar and tag.

'Douglas,' he said. 'Okay, Douglas. Where is he?'

THIRTY-EIGHT

It was Bobby Sharma who managed to track down Eleanor Clifton.

Luke had taken Douglas out of the flat so that the Forensic Team could start going through Bart Clifton's belongings. He was rubbing Douglas's belly while sitting on the stoop outside on the pavement when Sharma called with Eleanor on the line.

Luke put the call on speaker and Hana leaned in.

'It's my brother, isn't it?' Eleanor said.

'We think so, yes.'

'Your colleague told me about the Latin phrases. To the late are left the bones is something my father used to say constantly. He was terrible to my brother. Abusive.'

'In what context did he use this phrase?'

Eleanor Clifton then told them about her brother's childhood. Luke always hated this moment — a moment where he felt sympathy for a killer when he understood where and how the evil that lurked in him was formed.

Conrad Clifton thought his son was weak.

'There was no reason for him to think this. Bart might

have been a little bit sensitive, but he wasn't a small boy and he did well at sport. But my father seemed to dislike him. He thought he was teaching my brother to be tough, to learn how to cope with whatever life threw at him, but it ended up destroying him. My brother wasn't built to take this kind of abandonment. This kind of fear.'

'What did your father do?'

Hana and Luke listened intently as Eleanor described how their father would take Bart on the train into London when he was eight years old. The pretence for their mother was that Bart was being taken to wonderful London landmarks and cultural centres, but then the boy was left. He was left completely alone to find his way to whatever random meeting point in London that their father chose. And then he was threatened — if anyone ever approached him, Bart was to say that he was fine and did not need any help.

'Imagine that,' Eleanor said. 'A shy boy from the country-side, eight years old, barely able to read, and left in the centre of London. Sometimes it would take him hours and hours to find his way. Sometimes he was too terrified to leave the place where our father had put him and he waited until he was eventually collected by him again. When this happened, he was beaten when they got home. I used to hear it.'

The detectives looked at each other when Eleanor had finished describing this peculiar form of child abuse, realizing that the connection had never been about the people Bart Clifton murdered. The connection was about the places where he killed them.

'I put two and two together as soon as your colleague called. The British Museum, Liverpool Street Station, Hyde Park, Trafalgar Square. These are all places that my brother was left.'

'Eleanor,' said Luke, leaning towards the phone. 'It's extremely important that you tell us where else Bart was left by your father. Was there any one place that stands out as being the worst? Something that you know affected your brother more than the others?'

'Oh yes,' she said. 'The north side of London Bridge. Bart once stood there for eight hours.'

'Thank you.'

'Please don't hurt my brother.'

Luke and Hana hung up the call.

————

It was only fifteen minutes later when they had Bart Clifton surrounded on the north side of London Bridge, staring down into the Thames below.

Like many parts of the city, the bridge was quiet, but the streets running either side of the Thames had people going about their business — mothers with pushchairs, so many pedestrians racing around to get where they were going.

You could never fully clear a city of people. They knew he had a weapon and that he was more than happy to use it.

Luke and Hana watched the scene unfold from the back of the tactical van outside of Bart Clifton's flat, the screen had no sound, but they could hear the voice of Fiona Holland through the Commander's radio.

The bullet that went through Bart Clifton's chest killed him instantly when she gave the command.

THIRTY-NINE

S o much for Luke's intended week off that he had planned to spend at Bluffs Cottage. He was exhausted when he returned home on Sunday evening after the team had debriefed. Luke took off the clothes that had felt clean and fresh that morning but were now crumpled with his sweat and still slightly damp in some places. He would have felt better with a shower but was simply too tired, so he crawled straight into bed and slept soundly for over seven hours.

When he woke on Monday, he decided to take the day off. No one would blame him.

He texted Hana to tell her and got the thumbs up emoji back.

After he made his coffee, taking his time with a fresh bag of beans from the freezer, he took the mug back upstairs with him and placed it on the bedside table.

Then he did the thing that he had been avoiding for the past year and a half. He went into the closet and pulled out the box of Sadie's things.

These were the things that she had been using and reading

when she died. All of the mundane, simple things that make up a life. That when that life is suddenly gone, it becomes unbearable to see anymore.

Luke lifted the lid off the box and looked inside. He had forgotten some of the things that he and Hana and placed in this box so many months ago. Sadie's hand cream that usually sat next to the bed. Two paperbacks she was reading. An unfinished crossword puzzle. Receipts.

And Sadie's laptop.

Luke pulled it out and checked to see what kind of battery charger it was compatible with as the thing would need to be plugged in before it would turn on. No one had opened this laptop since about a fortnight after her death. Luke had needed to get a few things from it for all of the paperwork that comes with a death, but it had remained in hibernation since then. He had tried to take a look at it once before but his grief had overwhelmed him.

The laptop back up and running again, Luke sat cross-legged on the bed and logged in. He typed in Sadie's password — magnolia — not for the flower, but for the name of the street she lived on as a child.

Should Luke go into Sadie's email? He had looked at it on and off for the past eighteen months, mostly clearing away junk messages when they came in and unsubscribing from mailing lists. He had never seen anything that looked out of place.

The bookmark bar at the top of her browser screen only had four items. The weather, a social media account she used, their bank login screen, and something that was labelled Armchair Investigation.

He clicked on the bookmark and armchairinvestiga tion.com popped up onto the screen. It took Luke a moment to figure out what the website was for, but he soon realized that it was a forum for amateur internet sleuths to discuss true crime cases.

Luke couldn't help but smile to himself. Of course Sadie would have loved this website — she was constantly immersed in mystery books, fiction as well as the darker world of true crime. He used to tease her that this obsessive pastime was what made her fall in love with a detective.

Clicking through to the forum, Luke saw that the laptop was still signed in as a member of the forum. He looked at the account profile and saw that Sadie had called herself sleuth19.

Wondering what types of books or cases she had been discussing at the time she died, Luke began to read through Sadie's posts.

His blood ran cold.

This was not a fun game or a harmless way to pass the time.

Sadie and several other forum members were investigating a horrendous crime.

Three hours later when Luke could read no more of the posts, still sitting on the bed, still next to the coffee he had not touched which had turned cold many hours ago, he finally shut the laptop.

And he picked up the phone to call Hana.

IF YOU ENJOYED THE KILLING PAGES...

Please consider leaving a rating or a review on Amazon, it really helps new readers discover DCI Luke Wiley and the team.

DCI Luke Wiley returns in

A Spirit in the Dark

ABOUT THE AUTHOR

JAYE BAILEY is a writer living in London. She is a big fan of true crime and detective fiction and the characters of Luke, Sadie and Hana have been in her head for a long time. Jaye finally decided to put pen to paper and begin the DCI Luke Wiley series.

When she's not writing, Jaye loves to travel. When at home, her house seems to be the destination house of choice for all the neighbourhood cats and, in her humble opinion, she makes the best spaghetti bolognese on the planet. (Yes, she will send you the recipe.)

Find out more at: jayebaileybooks.com

TWO
YARDS

Printed in Great Britain
by Amazon

40762264R00142